MW01593837

ROSEANNA

by
VITI LEE TACKETT

**Based on the song *Roseanna*,
written and recorded by John Houston**

ISBN 0-939241-67-6

Copyright © 2000 by Viti Lee Tackett

Library of Congress Control Number: 00-090532

All rights reserved.

ROYAL FAMILY PUBLISHING
HIGH POINT, NC

Printed in the United States of America.

Faith Printing Company, Inc.
Taylors, SC 29687

All songs appearing by permission of and written
by John Houston/John Houston Publishing —
ASCAP.

Dedication

I gratefully dedicate this book to John Houston. His creation of Roseanna in the beautiful words of the song inspired me to write the book. His permission allowed me to write the book, and his first-hand knowledge of the aspects of the book kept me on tract and saved me many hours of research. His determination to not compromise the truth gave me the freedom to portray God as He really is: A Worker of Miracles. His unyielding belief that even impossible dreams will come true, if you don't give up, has challenged me to soar beyond my own horizons and reach for the stars.

Viti Lee Tackett began writing as a teenager; short stories, plays and poetry. She has been published in the fields of short stories, articles, and poetry. Her article, Woman, Her Role, was published in an international mission yearbook.

Viti felt the call into the teaching ministry, early in life, and has written and taught lessons in Ministers Retreats, Couples Retreats, Youth Camps, Kids Crusades, as well as in local churches.

ROSEANNA was written by the inspiration of God and under the direction of His Hand, with a prayer that each one who reads this book will be touched by God and your life changed forever.

Rev. Floyd V. Tackett

ACKNOWLEDGE MENTS

Thanks to Marty Rhyne, who promptly supplied information on tour buses (including pictures) when I requested it.

Thanks to Will Cassity, my computer expert, who not only taught me how to program my manuscript into the computer, but was always there to correct my mistakes (and they were many.)

Lillis (Jinks) Redd, my long-time friend, who is also an English teacher. Thanks, Jinks, for caring enough to take time out of your busy schedule to proofread my manuscript and steer me around the pitfalls of punctuation.

Thanks, Dr. C. Paul Willis and John Houston, for kindly giving your synopses of the book.

Thanks to Bill Coyne for supplying the picture for the front cover of the book.

Special thanks to my husband, Floyd, for all his help and support while I was writing the book and for his continued love and support.

Thanks to my family and friends for all their love and encouragement and especially their prayers.

There's a little white church down in bayou country deep in South Louisiana,

With a Holy Ghost preacher and a faithful congregation and a Cajun girl named Roseanna;

She plays guitar every Sunday morning cause the church doesn't have a piano,

And she sings so sweetly that the crowds will gather, people all the way from Alabama.

They come all the way from Alabama.

Sing Roseanna! Sing Roseanna! Sing Roseanna to the King of Kings!

Sing Roseanna! Sing Roseanna! Sing Roseanna to the King.

Chapter 1

Roseanna hurried along the footpath that lay between Turtle Creek and Toops Bayou. She was in one of her moods: the curse of her father, Grandma called it.

Ellis LeBlanc, a vagabond at heart, up and left his family seven years ago without so much as an explanation or good-bye. She hated the thought of being like him, but she couldn't deny it, she was her father's daughter.

The warmth of the sun caressed her cheeks as she reached her special place near the bayou, the place Daddy used to bring her to play the guitar and sing. She sat down on a big log and watched the old alligators as they slept lazily in the marsh, a safe distance away.

Roseanna sighed. "You were born to live in the bayou," she said as if they could hear her. "I wasn't. I don't belong here."

Roseanna knew the odds of getting out of the bayou. A Cajun girl grew up here, married young, had lots of kids and died without ever having tasted life in the outside world.

"That won't happen to me," she cried, "I won't let it." She strummed her guitar and sang softly:

"Down in the valley, the valley so low;

Hang your head over, hear the winds blow."

The tune matched her mood but the words spoke of someone else's sadness, not hers. Roseanna needed to express the way she felt; she strummed the tune and sang words that came from deep inside her heart:

2

"Down in the bayou, the willows they weep,

And tell a sad story, while the old gators sleep;

Of a young Cajun maiden whom the bayou can't keep,

She longs for her freedom with every heartbeat."

She sang the words over and over as if they would set her free, free to soar like the mighty eagle to heights above and beyond the boundaries of the bayou. For awhile Roseanna forgot about her surroundings and soared in her dreams to far-away places, magical places. Like Dorothy, she skipped down the yellow brick road that led to the glitter and bright lights of the big city and the life she so desperately yearned for.

"Roseanna!" Belle's voice rousted her from her reverie.

"I'm coming," she yelled, jumping to her feet and running to meet her sister.

"I knew I'd find you here," Belle said as Roseanna joined her. "Mama sent me to get you."

"What's up?" Roseanna asked.

"She didn't say."

"You messed up a perfectly wonderful dream," Roseanna scolded playfully. "But it's probably just as well, my dreams are just that—dreams."

"Dreams are important, Roseanna, don't ever give up on yours. Someday, they will come true, you'll see."

"Maybe," Roseanna reflected, then asked, "do you have dreams about your life, Belle?"

Belle laughed. "Yeah, I dream that one day a handsome Prince Charming will come riding up on his snow-white steed, swoop me up in his arms, and we'll ride off into the sunset to live happily ever after. Of course, if Prince Charming ever did come along, he'd take one look at you, tall and beautiful, with those big brown eyes and that million dollar smile, and I wouldn't stand a chance."

Roseanna giggled. "Can't you just see a handsome prince coming here to the bayou?"

They laughed at the prospect of that happening. Then they fell silent, each absorbed in her own thoughts.

Belle broke the silence. "Do you ever think about Daddy?" she asked thoughtfully.

"Yeah, when I play the guitar and sing I remember how it was before he left."

"You were his favorite, you know," Belle said. "He loved you special."

"Probably because I loved music the way he did. He started teaching me to play the guitar and write songs when I was about five. Write what you feel deep down inside," he told me. "Sing from your heart."

"That's one thing he did right," Belle said. "You sing like an angel."

"I feel good when I sing my songs in church," Roseanna replied. "It's like Heaven opens up and spills joy all over me."

"Some of that joy spills over on the rest of us," Belle remarked; then pausing a moment, she asked: "Do you know why Daddy left us?"

4

"To hear Grandma talk it was because he was a lazy no-good drifter. I can hear her now, telling how she warned Mama about him: 'Blanche, that man will bring you nothing but heartache'."

"She was right about that," Belle said. "I think I hate him most of all for what he did to Mama."

Roseanna nodded, then felt like a hypocrite, knowing she would leave in a minute, just like he did, if she got the chance.

"Mama, we're home," she called, as they walked through the open door into the house.

"Good," Mama said. "Mrs. Pecot is having a big to-do tonight and she needs me to help out. I'll stay and clean up afterwards so I'll be late getting home. I need you girls to fix supper and see to it that everyone gets their bath and gets to bed early. Tomorrow's a big day. The new preacher will be here."

"I wonder what he's like ," Roseanna pondered out loud.

"His family's from these parts but I don't remember them," Mama said. "They moved away several years ago, to Mississippi, I think."

Mrs. Pecot's chauffeur drove up just then and Mama left for work.

"I hate it cause Mama has to work so hard," Belle said as she watched the car drive away.

"Now that I've graduated high school, maybe I can get a job and help out," Roseanna said.

"Where's a seventeen year old girl gonna find work here?" Belle asked.

"I'm almost eighteen," Roseanna reminded her but she knew Belle was right, there were not many jobs for girls down here in bayou country.

"Maybe you can sell some of your songs," Belle suggested.

"You think people would pay money for my songs?"

"I don't know why not," Belle answered. "They're better than any I've heard, even the ones on the radio."

"Wouldn't that be something,'" Roseanna said, relishing the thought as they went into the kitchen to start supper.

Roseanna had to learn to cook when she was ten years old; that's when Daddy left and Mama went to work for Mrs. Pecot. The burden of taking care of the house and the younger children fell on Roseanna and Belle.

Soon, a pot of Mama's black-eyed peas was simmering on the stove, a pan of potatoes was frying in the iron skillet, and ears of corn from the garden were boiling in the big kettle. Belle sliced red-ripe tomatoes as Roseanna took a pan of cornbread from the oven.

"Supper's ready," Belle yelled and four girls of various sizes scurried to the table. After grace was said they devoured the food hungrily.

"I didn't know girls could eat so much," Roseanna teased as they passed their plates for seconds.

With everyone pitching in, the chores were done in record time, the baths were taken, and the younger children were in bed.

Roseanna and Belle sat for awhile, enjoying the quietness of the house and the gentle breeze flowing through the open windows.

"I'm going to miss Brother Trosclair," Roseanna said. "I'm not sure I can get used to a new preacher."

"Yeah, he's been preaching here since Mama was a little girl," Belle said, "but maybe the new preacher will be nice, too."

"With a name like Lefourche, he can't be all bad," Roseanna laughed. "We know he's not married but I wonder what he looks like."

"Our Prince Charming, maybe?" Belle mused.

Roseanna laughed again. "With our luck, most likely he'll be fat, bald and ugly."

Belle nodded. "You're probably right, but I'm going to bed and get my beauty sleep, just in case."

"As if you need it," Roseanna said, looking at her sister. Belle was tall and lanky with long brown hair, a shade lighter than Roseanna's, and soft brown eyes that sparkled when she laughed. Pretty now, one day she'd be a real beauty.

"Good-night," Roseanna said. She sat for awhile reflecting on the things around her. There was not much in the way of beauty here; the house was old and weather-beaten, furnished mostly with things Mama and Daddy had gotten when they got married. The blue floral couch and chairs were faded and worn by time and everyday wear and tear. A long homemade table, scarred and wobbly, with pieces of cardboard under the legs to steady it, held a lamp, the family Bible and a few knickknacks. An old sewing machine sat across one corner of the room. The bare floor was swept clean.

7

The house might be old and the furnishings meager but it was always neat and clean, Mama insisted on that; and there was always more than enough love to go around, Mama made sure of that too.

As Roseanna sat there, she felt that love wrap around her like a snug blanket and a warmth filled her heart that made her happy and content.

Tomorrow Roseanna's heart would once again become restless for the far-away places she dreamed of; but tonight home felt good.

Chapter 2

Roseanna sat looking at the mural of Jesus praying in the Garden which covered the front wall of the church behind the pulpit. It was a work of art, a thing of beauty. A young man traveling through their community years ago had painted it in exchange for a couple of months free room and board. He referred to himself as a 'starving artist' and when he finished the painting he signed it; "Just in case I ever become famous," he laughed and told them. They never saw him again but he did become famous and the mural became the pride of the congregation.

Roseanna felt a calmness whenever she looked at the painting. "That's what we need now," she mumbled looking around the sanctuary. Tension filled the air and lined the faces of the people as they waited and waited and waited.

Deacon LaPree paced up the middle aisle, across the front of the church and down the aisle again.

"Thirty minutes late," he growled snapping his pocket watch shut.

Being late went against the good deacon's grain; in fact, getting a young pastor went against his grain. He had made his feelings clear on that: "Young people today are not responsible, we need a seasoned minister," he had argued.

Now it appeared he might be right.

"He's coming! He's coming!" shouted the Chatelain twins stumbling in the door, each boy trying to be the first to tell the news.

Dust swelling up from the dirt road leading to the church did affirm that a car was coming, and since the rest of the congregation was already there, it had to be him.

"Everyone take your seats," the deacon snapped, walking to the door.

"Look at that fake smile," Belle whispered.

Every head turned in anticipation as the front door opened.

"Sorry we're so late," the two stately ladies whispered as they walked into the sanctuary.

"You're not as late as the preacher," Brother LaPree grumbled, shaking their hands.

"Miss Sarah and Miss Kathleen," Belle whispered. "Wonder what they're doing back today. It's only been a couple of weeks since they were here."

"They probably couldn't wait to meet the new minister," Roseanna said.

Miss Sarah and Miss Kathleen, two sisters from Grand Bay, Alabama, made the long trip down to the bayou every six weeks or so and even though they had relatives living in the area, they confessed that the main reason they came so often was to hear Roseanna sing.

Roseanna waved to the ladies as they sat down on the pew opposite her.

"Speaking of the new minister, reckon something happened?" Belle remarked.

"Maybe he changed his mind about coming to the bayou," Roseanna said. She could understand if he had.

"Let's sing," someone suggested and Roseanna walked to the platform. She picked up her guitar and sat down on the stool put there especially for her.

"Everyone stand and sing Amazing Grace," she said and started singing. Soon the tension lifted as folks got in the spirit of worship.

There were no windows where Roseanna was sitting and she began to feel hot and flushed. The small oscillating fan offered little relief. Belle noticed her discomfort and brought a glass of water from the back.

"Let Roseanna sing one of her songs," Miss Kathleen suggested between choruses.

Everyone nodded and sat down.

Roseanna adjusted her guitar, took a swallow of water and started strumming. "I'm going to sing, "Sunshine". I hope you enjoy it."

The side door burst open and a tall dark-haired young man bolted into the sanctuary.

"Sorry I'm late, folks," he said breathlessly. "My car broke down about twenty miles down the road and I had to hitch a ride here. Oh, by the way, I'm Bradley Lefourche, your new minister."

Waves of applause and shouts of joy welcomed him.

Roseanna sat stunned. She had never dreamed he'd be so good-looking. She blushed as he turned and looked at her.

"I'm sorry," he apologized. "I interrupted your song. Please go ahead and sing."

Roseanna's mind went blank. Which song was she going to sing? What were the words? She took a sip of water and cleared her throat. "Lord, help me," she prayed silently. The words came back to her and she sang in a voice clear and sweet:

> *Everyone's soul has been a little undone sometimes,*
>
> *Everyone's heart has been broken before;*
>
> *And everyone's tears fall like rain sometimes,*
>
> *We could all use a little sunshine,*
>
> *We could use a little sunshine,*
>
> *We could all use a little sunshine today.*
>
>
> *Everyone's cried over someone else sometimes,*
>
> *Sooner or later everyone feels the same old pain;*
>
> *And everyone wants to be relieved sometimes,*
>
> *We could all use a little sunshine,*
>
> *We could all use a little sunshine,*
>
> *We could all use a little sunshine today.*

Everyone cries out to Jesus sometimes,

Sooner or later it shall surely be;

Just don't wait until the end of time,

We could all use a little sunshine,

We could use a little sunshine,

We could use a little sunshine today.

As Roseanna stood to go back to her seat the young minister reached out and took her hand. "I've never heard anyone sing like you," he said. "That was beautiful."

Roseanna's knees buckled under her. She reached out to steady herself but instead she fainted dead away, right into the arms of young Bradley Lefourche.

The minister held her with one hand and took a clean white handkerchief from his pocket with the other hand. He dipped it in the glass of water and gently stroked her face.

"Give her room to breathe," he cautioned as folks crowded the platform.

Roseanna stirred in his arms. "She's coming around," he said. "Everyone please go back to your seats."

Roseanna opened her eyes and looked into the deepest blue eyes she had ever seen. They were like pools of clear sparkling water that rippled into her very soul.

"I've got to get up," she mumbled.

"Careful now," the preacher said, "don't try to stand yet."

"I'm fine," she insisted. "I just need to sit down."

"Where were you sitting?" Belle raised her hand and he picked Roseanna up and carried her to the pew and sat her down gently.

"Keep this on your forehead," he said handing her the handkerchief. "Are you sure you're all right?"

Roseanna nodded. "I'm f-fine-really," she stammered,

"Well, if you're sure," he said and walked back to the pulpit. "It looks like the crisis is over so we'll go on with the service. Turn in your Bibles to the thirteenth chapter of First Corinthians. My message today is on Love."

Loud amen's and hallelujah's resounding through the sanctuary was proof that he was preaching a powerful sermon but Roseanna didn't hear a word he said.

Humiliation consumed her. It burned through her like the hot desert sun beating down relentlessly, scorching her innermost being.

"I've got to get out of here," she whispered to Belle. "Tell Mama we're leaving."

Brother Lefourche stopped momentarily when the girls walked out.

"She's okay," Mama said, "just needed some fresh air."

Once they were outside Belle asked teasingly, "Don't you want to stay and be properly introduced to the new preacher?"

"I can never face him again," Roseanna cried. "I made a complete fool of myself. Me, an almost grown woman, fainting like that."

"Right into his arms," Belle laughed.

"It's not funny. I've never been so embarrassed in all of my life."

"Everyone knows you fainted from the heat," Belle said.

"I wonder," Roseanna mused. "If I tell you something you must promise never to tell a living soul."

"Cross my heart and hope to die," Belle promised.

"I'm not sure it was the heat that caused me to faint," Roseanna confessed, "I think it was the preacher. The minute he walked through that door, I lost it."

"You and every other girl there," Belle said.

"But they didn't faint in his arms," Roseanna mumbled. "I can't go back in there and face him."

"Let's go over to Grandma's and have dinner on the table when they get home," Belle suggested.

"Wonder why Grandma is using her good tablecloth and napkins," Roseanna said when they walked in the house.

"Treating us like royalty, I guess," Belle answered.

They had finished in the kitchen and were setting the table when they heard voices outside.

"Set another place girls. We've got company," Grandma announced as she walked in the door.

Roseanna flinched when the minister followed Grandma inside.

"Are you all right?" he asked her with concern in his voice.

"Yes, I'm fine," Roseanna muttered and not able to face him she hurried off to the kitchen. Belle followed her.

"How could Grandma do this to me?" Roseanna whispered angrily. "I can't sit at the same table with him. I get sick just thinking about it."

"Maybe it won't be so bad," Belle said. "Grandma's table is long, so just..."

"Come on girls," Grandma called. "Everyone's here. We're ready to eat. Brother Lefourche, you sit there." She pointed to the head of the table.

Roseanna quickly sat down in a chair on the side, at the opposite end of the table.

"I wouldn't think of taking your place," the minister told Grandma. "I'll sit here." He pulled out the chair next to Roseanna and sat down. "I don't believe we've been properly introduced," he said extending his hand. "I'm Bradley Lefourche."

"Roseanna," she mumbled, feebly shaking his hand.

"Roseanna, I enjoyed your singing so much. I understand you wrote the song."

She nodded.

"Pastor, say Grace please, so we can eat before the food gets cold," Grandma said.

"Let's join hands," he said offering up a prayer of thanksgiving.

Roseanna wished she could excuse herself and leave the table, but Mama would never stand for such rudeness. She had to make it through dinner somehow. She was glad when the prayer ended and the minister let go of her hand.

"This is the best gumbo I've ever tasted," Brother Lefourche exclaimed. "What's your secret?"

"First you make the roux," Grandma said.

A roar of laughter went up.

"Everyone knows that, Grandma," young Ellie grunted.

"And that's all you'll get from her," Belle added. "Grandma doesn't share her gumbo secrets with anyone, not even us."

"As long as I have breath in me, I'll make the gumbo for this family," Grandma asserted. "Before I die I promise to pass my secrets on to you girls."

"Thank you for at least sharing your gumbo with me," the preacher said, laughing.

"I'll do the dishes," Roseanna volunteered as soon as the last bite of dessert vanished.

"No, there's plenty of us to take care of the dishes. You show the preacher around," Grandma insisted. "No one knows the bayou like you."

"Grandma, I'm sure he has other things to do," Roseanna protested.

"I'd love to see the bayou," he said, "and I'm sure I couldn't find a better tour guide."

It was settled, Roseanna knew it. When Grandma made up her mind there was no need to argue.

"Stop by the house and change into some cooler clothes," Mama said.

"We wouldn't want you fainting again," Grandma added, winking at them.

Roseanna slipped into a bright yellow sun-dress and quickly braided her dark brown hair into one long braid. She put on a pair of blue canvas sneakers and taking a quick glance in the mirror, she joined the preacher in the living room. "All ready," she said.

"I hope you don't mind, it's too hot outside for these," he said hanging his jacket and tie across a chair and rolling up his shirt sleeves.

Roseanna felt ill-at-ease walking beside him. This morning weighed heavy on her mind; like the smell of mothballs it clung in the air stifling her. She had to do something before she choked.

"Brother Lefourche," she mumbled, "I'm sorry about this morning, fainting like that."

"Don't apologize. I kinda liked it." He grinned. "It's not every day that a pretty young lady falls right into my arms."

Roseanna blushed a deep red.

"However, there is one thing you can do," he continued, "stop calling me Brother Lefourche, call me Brad."

"But you're our pastor."

"I'm not much older than you, Roseanna. Please don't make me feel like a grandpa by calling me Brother Lefourche," he said, moaning, holding his back and hobbling around.

Roseanna laughed. That laughter broke the tension and cleared the air. She finally relaxed and soon they were chatting like old friends.

"Let's rest for awhile," she said when they had covered most of the bayou area. She had saved this place for last. "This is my special place," she told him, "the place I come to when I need to be alone, to play the guitar and sing, to write my songs or just to sit and dream."

"I can see why," he said. "It's so peaceful here."

"Brother-er-Brad, what made you decide to become a preacher?" she asked as they sat down on a big log.

"It's a calling," he answered. "But I think I wanted to be a preacher long before I got the call. It started when I was six years old at a camp meeting in Popularville, Mississippi. Even though I was just a boy, I remember it like it was yesterday. The camp meetings were held in the hottest part of summer, but that didn't dampen the enthusiasm. Folks would come from miles around. They'd bring their tents and stay for the entire revival. I remember the brush arbors entwined with honeysuckle in bloom and how their sweet fragrance filled the air. I can still see the Spanish Moss waving from tall oak trees and hear the shouts of hallelujah's and stanza's of Amazing Grace resounding across the countryside. You should have heard those old time preachers telling us how that Jesus was coming soon, and if sinners wanted to be ready, they'd better change their ways. Grandma sang Sweet Hour of Prayer with such conviction, that sinners would run to the altar to repent. At the end of the revival, there was a baptizing in Pearl River. We'd sit up on the hill and watch and listen as Grandpa read from the gospels, mostly Luke and John, how Jesus was baptized in the Jordan River, and then after all the folks who had been converted were baptized we'd pray and sing until the sun went down."

He paused a moment then went on, "Those memories of when I was six years old is what brought me back to the Lord. When I was in high school, I rebelled against everything I had been taught. The day I graduated, I left home and rambled around the country for a few years. I did some things I'm not proud of. Then a couple of years ago those memories from the past overtook me, and I gave my heart to the Lord again. That's when He called me to preach. I've been so busy preparing for the ministry, I haven't had a chance to go back home. I have a burning desire to attend another camp meeting there and sing some of those wonderful hymns with friends I knew back then." He paused again. "I've never shared this with anyone," he said. "Thanks for listening."

"I'm glad you shared it with me," she said softly.

"The sun's almost down behind the horizon so we'd better head for home," Brad said reluctantly.

"It's a good thing we're not having church tonight, or you'd be late again," Roseanna teased.

"I don't know how the good deacon would take to that," Brad said grinning.

"You noticed? Don't worry, he won't give you trouble with Grandma on your side. You made a hit with her, you know."

"I hope it runs in the family. I want to make a hit with you, Roseanna," he said helping her to her feet.

Their eyes met. Their gaze lingered. Roseanna thought he was going to kiss her. She wanted him to.

He stepped back and took her hand.

Holding his hand felt right, her world felt right, even the bayou felt right. And as she held on to that strong gentle hand, Roseanna knew her heart had found a home.

Chapter 3

The sun shining brightly through the window woke Roseanna.

Belle stirred in the bed beside her. "What time is it?" she asked yawning.

"I think it's late. Angelina's already up," Roseanna said, nodding toward the other bed in the room.

"Well, she didn't stay awake half the night talking about 'Mr. Wonderful'," Belle teased.

"Yesterday really happened, didn't it? It wasn't a dream," Roseanna mused.

"Yes, it happened, beginning with you fainting in the preacher's arms."

"In front of the whole church," Roseanna added. "I'd like to forget that part."

Ellie came running into the room. "Preacher's here to see Roseanna," she announced.

"Oh, no," Roseanna fretted, glancing in the mirror. "I look a mess—my hair—I'm not even dressed."

"Relax, I'll go out and keep him company while you make yourself beautiful. I don't mind him seeing me in my ratty old housecoat," Belle said laughing.

Roseanna grabbed a pair of jeans and a blue printed top. She brushed her hair and let it fall loose down her back. "That will have to do," she said, taking a deep breath.

"Good morning," Brad said when she walked into the room. "I'm sorry to come by so early, but I'm going into town and thought you might want to come along; that is, if it's okay with your mother."

"Sure, it's okay," Mama said. "I'm certain Belle can handle things around here today."

Belle nodded.

"Do I need to change clothes?" Roseanna asked.

Brad grinned. "Those clothes are fine, but you might want to wear some shoes."

Roseanna looked at her bare feet. In her haste to get dressed she had forgotten her shoes. Blushing, she hurried to the bedroom and slipped her feet into a pair of white sandals. "Now, I'm ready," she said, still blushing.

"I've got Earl's truck," Brad explained as they walked outside. "He towed my car in and loaned me this truck til he gets it fixed. I hope you don't mind a bumpy ride."

"Not at all," she assured him.

He opened the door for her, ran around to the driver's side, and they were on their way.

Roseanna glanced over at him. The blue pullover shirt he was wearing made his eyes sparkle even more than before.

"You look great," she blurted out, and blushed when she realized she'd said the words out loud.

"Aw, shucks, ma-am, all the ladies tell me that," he said making a joke of it.

Roseanna laughed. He sure had a knack for making her feel better.

"Let's sing," he suggested and broke into stanzas of "Row, row, row your boat, gently down the stream." He sang slightly off key, but that didn't matter. Roseanna joined in and kept the rounds going.

Before they realized it they had pulled into the city limits.

"We'll go by the hardware store first," Brad said, "then what would you like to do?"

"I could show you the town," she suggested.

"That sounds great." As soon as he took care of his business, they started on their tour.

Roseanna showed him lovely old homes, they walked through the park looking at the statues, the charming fountain, and the colorful flowers growing there. Then they toured a local museum.

"All that walking made me hungry," Brad said. "Are you ready to eat?"

"Yes," she replied quickly. Her stomach reminded her that she hadn't eaten breakfast "I know a place where they make terrific burgers."

"Sounds good," he said, and soon they were hungrily devouring burgers, fries, and chocolate milkshakes.

"It's been a good day," Brad remarked as they pulled into Roseanna's yard late that afternoon.

"It's been a great day," she agreed.

"Roseanna! Preacher!" ten year old Aimee yelled, running up to the truck. "Grandma's in a tizzy. She needs you to come to her house right now!"

Brad revved the engine and spun out onto the road. In less than a minute they pulled in at Grandma's house.

She was out in the yard waving a broom through the air.

"Quick, up on the roof!" she yelled, handing Brad the broom. "Clean the gutter, don't leave one leaf or a drop of water anywhere. Hurry!" Then her attention turned to Roseanna. "Child, empty all the containers that have water in them."

"Grandma," Roseanna chided knowingly.

"Don't argue, just do it!" Grandma snapped.

"It's all clean," Brad said, huffing, as he climbed down from the roof. "Now tell me what's going on."

"Couchemal!" Grandma cried.

Brad shrugged his shoulders.

"It's an old Cajun superstition," Roseanna explained. "Babies that die before they are baptized

25

become couchemals or evil spirits and lurk around like lesser ghosts. To keep the couchemals away you must drain the contents of the roof's rain-gathering cistern and any other containers of liquid where the couchemal might settle. Did I leave anything out, Grandma?"

Grandma shook her head.

"A superstition?" Brad couldn't believe his ears. "Me, a minister of the gospel, got up on that roof and cleaned out the gutter all because of a superstition? Sister, we've got to have a talk."

Grandma mumbled under her breath.

"Whose baby died?" Roseanna asked.

"A family over in the next parish, but who knows how far those evil spirits can travel," Grandma replied nervously.

"Sister Gautier," Brad said tenderly, "it's sad that the baby died but I can assure you that his spirit is with God and not floating around down here."

"How do you know that for sure?" Grandma asked.

"The Bible tells me," the young minister answered. "In Ezekiel it says: 'All souls are mine, the soul that sinneth, it shall die.' That new-born baby had no sin, so would a loving God let a sinless soul become a evil spirit?"

"I suppose not," Grandma muttered.

As Roseanna and Brad drove away they saw Grandma waving the broom through the air again.

"Better safe than sorry is her motto," Roseanna said laughing,

"I can see I've got a lot of work to do here," Brad said, shaking his head.

Roseanna spent a lot of time that week at her special place. With guitar and notebook in hand, she disappeared for hours at a time. She was working on something special for the Sunday morning service. She finished it on Saturday and kept it a secret, even from Belle.

Roseanna and Belle met a stranger as they walked to church the next morning. He looked hot and tired.

"Good morning," he said pausing a moment. "My car ran out of gas over on the highway. I passed a gas station on this road but no one was there."

"That's Earl's place and he's closed on Sundays," Roseanna told him.

"Do you know where I can find him?"

"Sure, right there in the church," Belle answered.

"Thank you, girls," the man said. "I'll get him to take me by his gas station and then to my car."

"Earl, this man needs to talk to you," Roseanna said, sitting down on the pew in front of Earl.

"I've got to hear this," Belle whispered, sitting down by Roseanna.

"I'm Robert Scott," the man said, "my car ran out of gas over on the highway. I understand you own a gas station."

"Yep."

"I need you to take me by your station, pick up some gasoline and then drive me back to my car."

"I'll be happy to oblige."

"Great!" the man exclaimed.

Earl sat there.

"Come on," the man urged. "I'm on my way back to Nashville and I'm in a hurry."

"Can't come right now," Earl said.

"Why not?" the man fumed.

"Cause church is fixin' to start," Earl replied.

"So, what does that have to do with anything?" Mr Scott sneered. "I told you I'm in a hurry. You're a business man, I'll make it worth your while. I'll give you an extra fifty dollars."

"Can't do it," Earl said.

"Okay, a hundred dollars." The man's face flushed an angry red.

"No way," Earl told him, "but if you'll wait til church is over, I'll be glad to help you at no charge except for the gasoline."

The man shook with anger. He got right in Earl's face and hissed through clenched teeth, "What kind of people are you down here in this bayou country turning down good money because of a church service?"

"Christians," Earl replied.

Roseanna and Belle snickered under their breaths as the man sat down, seething, on the pew beside Earl.

Roseanna played the guitar for the singing, but her mind was on her surprise. She sat impatiently through the service, waiting 'til time for her song. She was not the only anxious one; Mr. Scott looked at his watch every few seconds.

Finally, Brad called on Roseanna to sing.

"I have a surprise for you folks today and a special surprise for one of you. I've written a new song. I hope you like it.

Spanish Moss waved gently from tall oak trees,

Amazing Grace rolled on the breeze;

And the tents were pitched on old campground,

And hallelujah's were all around,

Hallelujah's were all around.

Brush Arbor honeysuckles bloomed,

And we all heard, Christ is coming soon;

And Grandma she sang Sweet Hour of Prayer,

I was six years old when I was there,

I was six years old when I was there.

Pearl River ran down through Popularville,

We watched baptizings from on top of the hill;

And Grandpa he would read from Luke and John,

And we prayed and sang til the setting of sun.

Well, I'd love to go back home again,

And see some long forgotten friends;

And sing some old familiar hymns,

Like finding pockets full of gems,

It would be just like finding pockets full of gems.

Those southern summer days were so fine,

They brought on sweet revival time;

Camp meeting preaching, Lord, it filled the air,

I was six years old when I was there,

I was six years old when I was there.

Spanish Moss waved gently from tall oak trees,

Amazing Grace rolled on the breeze;

And the tents they were pitched out on old campground,

And hallelujah's they were all around.

And Brush Arbor honeysuckles they bloomed,

And we all heard Christ is coming real soon;

And Grandma she sang Sweet Hour of Prayer,

I was six years old when I was there,

I was six years old when I was there.

As Roseanna sang the congregation sat in rapt attention, Brad wiped tears from his eyes and the business man from Nashville didn't look at his watch one time.

"Thank you, Roseanna," Brad said, squeezing her hand, "that was a wonderful surprise. Excuse my tears, folks," he said to the congregation. "That song is about my home in Mississippi and Roseanna has captured it so beautifully, I almost feel as if I'm back there,"

After the service ended, the man from Nashville lingered long enough to speak to Roseanna. "That was good singing, little lady. Did I hear you right—you wrote the song?"

Roseanna nodded.

"Do you write a lot of songs?"

"Every one she sings," Belle bragged.

"Well, I'm glad I stayed," he said. "It's worth being a little late to get to hear you sing."

"Thank you, sir," Roseanna said, smiling at him.

Hours later as he drove along Interstate 20, Robert Scott was still humming Roseanna's song. He picked up the car phone and dialed.

"Prince residence," a voice said.

"Maurice, this is Robert Scott. Let me speak to J.T."

Chapter 4

It was Mid-July. The bayou sweltered in the hot summer sun. The alligators had gone underwater to escape the blazing heat. Only Roseanna ventured out to the bayou. She needed to be in her special place to think.

She had spent every free minute with Brad for the past few weeks. Now he was back home in Mississippi at Camp Meeting and she felt lost without him.

In his absence doubts flooded her mind. Did he really love her? He acted as if he did but he had never actually said he loved her, he had never even kissed her. She loved him, but did he love her back?

She picked a flower, and as she plucked the petals she chanted; "Loves me, loves me not. Loves me, loves me not." She continued until only one petal was left—"loves me not." She threw the stem down. "What do you know," she snorted in disgust. "I've got to stop this, Brad will be home tonight and things will be right again."

Mama and the girls had left for church when Roseanna got home. She grabbed a bite to eat and dressed hurriedly.

Most of the Wednesday night crowd was already inside when she walked into the church yard. Brad was coming out of the parsonage. She waited for him.

He looked all around. There was no one in sight.

"I've wanted to do this since the first time I saw you," he said. He pulled her close and kissed her, a long, sweet, tender kiss.

They heard the giggling before they saw the Chatelain twins peeking around the corner of the church.

"I should have known," Brad said and dashed off to catch them.

They were quicker than him and ran into the church. They skipped up the aisle chanting: "Preacher kissed Roseanna! Preacher kissed Roseanna!" Their mother hissed at them and they sat down.

Roseanna wanted to strangle them. She sat down on the back pew, too embarrassed to look at anyone.

Brad walked to the pulpit. "Guilty as charged," he said. "I kissed her. I'm not sorry and I'm not going to apologize. I love that girl and I'm going to marry her if she'll have me." He paused a moment and looked at Roseanna. "You will have me, won't you, Roseanna?"

Everyone turned and looked at her, waiting for the answer.

Roseanna burst into tears and ran out the door.

"Pray folks," Brad said, racing after her.

"Roseanna, please listen," he pleaded when he caught up with her. "I'm so sorry. I'd sooner die than hurt you. I shouldn't have blurted it out in front of everyone. I should have done it right. I meant to. I practiced and practiced, then my big mouth got in the way. I love you more than life itself. Please forgive me and tell me I still have a chance with you, and sweetheart, please don't cry." He wiped the tears from her face.

"I can't help it," she sobbed. "That was the most beautiful proposal I ever heard."

"You liked it?" Brad asked, stunned.

"Of course I liked it and of course I'll have you, now and forever."

"Hallelujah!" Brad yelled, picking her up and swinging her around.

"I think that's a yes," Grandma said beaming as cheers went up from the congregation who had gathered outside. They rushed forward to congratulate the happy couple.

"Way to go, boy," Deacon LaPree exclaimed, slapping Brad on the back. He didn't seem to mind that the church service had been totally ruined.

Things calmed down after a bit and folks went home.

"There's one thing I don't understand," Brad said later as they sat in front of her house, "since you liked my proposal, why did you run out of the church crying?"

"It's a girl thing," Roseanna explained, laughing. "You'll get used to it."

Later, when he walked her to the door, they clung to each other reluctant to say good-night.

"I've really got to go in now," she said giving him one final kiss. She watched out the window as he drove away. Then she tip-toed into the bedroom not wanting to disturb her sisters.

"I'm awake," Belle said. "I couldn't go to sleep til you got home."

"You're turning into a regular old mother hen," Roseanna laughed.

"I've been thinking," Belle continued, "I know Brad is terrific but are you sure this is what you want? What about your dreams, can you just forget them?"

"I guess a part of me will always have those dreams," Roseanna confessed. "But what I have with Brad is real and it's right; we have our own dreams now. Don't worry little sister, I've never been happier."

"Good," Belle said. "now maybe I can get some sleep."

"You'll be my maid-of-honor, of course," Roseanna said dreamily. "Ellie will be my flower girl. Angelina, Jolee and Aimee will be bridesmaids. I can see it all now."

"Sounds lovely, but go to bed," Belle said yawning. "Tomorrow's almost here."

"Maybe I'll write a song for the wedding," Roseanna continued, ignoring her sister's request.

"Turn out the light and go to sleep please," Belle pleaded, covering her head with her pillow.

Roseanna turned off the light but sleep was far from her. Her mind whirled with thoughts of Brad and plans for the future.

"Roseanna Lefourche," she whispered. That sounded good. "Mrs Bradley Lefourche." That sounded even better. She smiled as she thought of her life as Brad's wife.

Sleep finally overtook her and she dreamed of floating on a cloud over far-away places dressed in a wedding gown.

"I guess we'd better start making plans," Mama said next morning.

"Just something simple, Mama," Roseanna told her, knowing there was not much money for such things.

"My little girl is going to have a nice wedding if I have to work overtime to pay for it."

"I don't want you doing that, Mama. If there was only a way that I could earn some money."

"There may be," Mama said. "Mrs. Pecot is having a really big party tomorrow night. She'll need extra help. Would you and Belle like to help out?"

"Yes!" they exclaimed. A trip to the Pecot mansion was a treat within itself; to get paid for it was like extra icing on the cake.

The next two days were filled with making plans for the wedding. Brad brought over addresses of his family and friends to be added to the guest list.

"I hope they like me," Roseanna said worriedly.

"They'll love you," he assured her, looking at his watch. "I've got to be going. I'll miss you tonight, sweetheart. Don't work too hard at Mrs Pecot's party," he added, giving her a lingering good-bye kiss.

When Roseanna stepped into the Pecot mansion that night, it was like stepping into another world. She stood for a moment awed by it's beauty.

Crystal chandeliers hung from the ceiling in the massive living and dining rooms. Brass candelabras holding brightly lit candles were scattered throughout. Impressive paintings adorned the walls. Vases of fresh cut flowers added fragrance and warmth.

"I could get used to this," she whispered to Belle.

A worried look crossed Belle's face. "Let's go help Mama," she suggested.

They shined the silver with soft polishing cloths and wiped the long-stemmed crystal glasses until they sparkled. They placed hors d'oeuvres and petits fours onto silver trays, ready to be served to the guests.

Soon the party was in full swing. Happy voices and laughter drifted back to the kitchen.

"Sounds as if everyone is having a good time," Roseanna remarked.

Belle nodded as Mrs. Pecot walked in. She looked grim.

"Roseanna, I need your help," she said. "The man who was to provide the entertainment tonight has taken ill and can't come. Will you sing for us?"

"I-I don't know," Roseanna's voice faltered. "I'm not dressed for a party. I don't have my guitar."

"Jiles can drive you to get your things," Mrs. Pecot offered.

"Most of my songs are religious," Roseanna explained. "I don't know any party songs."

Mrs. Pecot laughed. "A little religion won't hurt any of us. Your songs will be fine."

"Okay, I'll give it a try," Roseanna said hesitantly, hoping it wasn't a mistake.

"Hurry along, dear," Mrs. Pecot urged, "we don't want to keep the guests waiting."

Roseanna returned shortly looking lovely in a soft pink dress. Mrs. Pecot made the announcement.

"There's been a slight change in plans. Our scheduled entertainment can't be here but we have a special treat for you. A young girl from right here on the bayou is going to sing for us. Not only does she sing like an angel; she writes all of her songs. Give a warm welcome to Roseanna."

A polite round of applause went up.

Roseanna looked the crowd over. It was a gathering of the rich and famous. Everyone who was anyone socially was sitting out there. Her heart pounded, her hands trembled. She wanted to run.

Mama and Belle stood in the back of the room. They smiled at her as if to say, "You can do it."

Roseanna strummed hard on her guitar to be heard over the buzz of the crowd. She sang shakily at first, then in a voice strong and clear.

*Everyone's soul has been a little undone,
sometimes,*

Everyone's heart has been broken before;

The crowd grew quiet; tears glistened as
Roseanna sang of the hurts and pain everyone feels, and
of the sunshine everyone needs at one time or another.
When the song ended, the room exploded in a roar of
applause. Shouts of "More! More!" kept her singing
for over an hour.

Performing here, before this audience she felt
exuberant, alive. Something stirred deep inside her;
feelings she thought were dead rekindled within her.

"Mama! Belle! They liked me!" Roseanna
exclaimed running into the kitchen as waves of applause
rang out through the house.

"Of course they liked you," Belle said, hugging
her sister.

"I'm so proud of my little girl," Mama said,
wiping tears of joy from her eyes.

"My guests and I want you to have this,
Roseanna," Mrs. Pecot said later, placing an envelope in
her hand.

"Thank you," Roseanna said, "and thank you
for asking me to sing."

"The pleasure was ours, I assure you," Mrs
Pecot said.

When they got home Roseanna opened the
envelope. There was money inside, lots of money, more
money than Roseanna had ever seen. She counted it.

"I can't believe it," she gasped, "there's over a
thousand dollars in here!"

Mama and Belle rushed over to see.

As Roseanna held the money in her hand she felt an exhilaration different from any she'd ever felt before.

Later, lying in bed, she still tingled with excitement, "A thousand dollars for one night's work," she whispered to Belle.

"That's enough to pay for the wedding," Belle said.

The Wedding. Roseanna felt a pang of guilt; she had not once thought of the wedding, or of Brad since she stepped into the Pecot mansion tonight. Tears stung her eyes as she fought the feelings inside her.

She needed Brad now. She needed to be in his arms, she needed to feel the tenderness of his kiss, the strength of his love.

"Tomorrow he will be here and all these feelings will fade away," she told herself as she drifted off into a troubled sleep.

Chapter 5

Roseanna was deep in thought as she and Belle walked to church Sunday morning. She was still shaken by the feelings that had surfaced inside her at Mrs Pecot's party.

"You want to talk about it?" Belle asked, sensing Roseanna's mood.

"There's nothing to talk about. In a couple of months I'll marry Brad and everything will be fine."

"Are you sure?" Belle questioned.

"Am I sure of my love for Brad or his for me? I've never been more sure of anything in my life."

"Are you sure loving him is enough? You've had dreams of a life outside the bayou forever. Those dreams are a part of you, can you just forget them?"

"I've got to," Roseanna said. "They were foolish out of reach dreams. My happiness is with Brad."

"What about Mrs. Pecot's party?" Belle asked point blank.

"I'll admit it was exciting and I got caught up in the thrill of the moment, but the next day when Brad held me in his arms and kissed me, those feelings flew right out the window. Don't worry , Belle, this is right for me."

Their conversation was cut short when a car whizzed by them in a swirl of dust.

"Wow!" Belle exclaimed. "I've never seen a car that big!"

"It's a limousine," Roseanna explained. "Funeral homes have them, but I don't think that one is from a funeral home; it's white and going too fast."

"Wonder what it's doing here?" Belle asked.

"Probably lost," Roseanna answered as they walked into the church yard and saw the car parked there.

The door of the limousine opened and a tall man stepped out. He was dressed in a very expensive western suit and cowboy boots. His black hair was full and well-groomed. A dimple, set in the middle of his chin, broke the smoothness of his dark-tone face. Eyes, deep set and black as midnight, were shaded by thick black eyebrows and long eyelashes.

"Whew," Belle sighed, "Prince Charming has come to the bayou."

"And what a handsome Prince Charming he is," Roseanna added. "The ones in the fairy tales can't hold a candle to him."

"Remember, you're engaged," Belle told her.

"I know, but he's still handsome."

"Look at those diamonds," Belle drooled as he put his hands on the car door.

"You coming in, Maurice?" the man asked his driver, a distinguished looking black man, who nodded and smiled pleasantly. The two men walked into the church without ever noticing Roseanna and Belle.

"Looks like he's staying for church," Belle whispered.

"What do you make of that?" Roseanna reflected.

"We have visitors today," Brad announced later, glancing at the cards in his hand. "John Taylor Prince and Maurice Alexander all the way from Tennessee. We welcome you, gentlemen, and invite you to worship with us."

The men nodded politely.

Who was this handsome Prince Charming and what was he doing down here in bayou country? Roseanna stole a glance at him as she played for the singing. He looked uncomfortable. Why was he here when he obviously felt out of place.

Maurice joined in as the Spirit moved through the hearts of the people and shouts of praise and worship filled the sanctuary, but Prince Charming turned pale and squirmed in the pew.

"He's gonna faint "Roseanna mumbled under her breath and wondered why he stayed when he evidently didn't want to be here.

"It's time for Roseanna's song," Brad announced later .

The man leaned forward in the pew; for the first time he seemed interested.

"I'm going to sing, "Were I An Eagle". It's new, I hope you like it."

Were I an eagle He'd be there,

Some place distant in the air;

Calling the winds to brace my wings,

Were I an eagle I would sing.

Or just a flower in the field,

He'd help me grow that I might yield;

Another dolphin in the sea,

He'd fill the oceans just for me.

I could be anything at all,

Something great or something small;

Yet there is nothing that I might be,

Where Jesus lives that he cannot see.

And I could hide my face in shame,

And let the whole world do the same;

Still He'd see every teardrop fall,

And stick around to dry them all.

Jesus loves me yes I know,

He gave His life to tell me so;

And yes, I finally realized,

It was for me that Jesus died.

And while I'm singing here today,

With all my heart I'd like to say;

I've been redeemed, I'm born again,

Yes, I know Jesus, He's my best Friend.

And I could be anyone at all,

Someone great or someone small;

Yet there is no one that I could be,

Where Jesus lives that He cannot see;

And I could hide my face in shame,

And let the whole world do the same;

Still He'd see every teardrop fall,

And stick around to dry them all.

Were I an eagle He'd be there.

When the service ended the man walked up to Roseanna. "I've heard about you, girl," he said. "I've come to change your life."

"You talking to me?" she asked puzzled.

"Yes," the man said. "My car's outside. Let me take you to lunch, we need to talk."

Roseanna's head was in the clouds. Was she hearing right—a chance to ride in that limousine? What she wouldn't give for that. Stark reality brought her back down to earth. Why would a rich important man like Prince Charming want to talk to her? How could he possibly change her life? What was really going on?

"Excuse me," she said, "I'll be right back." She rushed off to find Brad. He'd know what to do.

"He's counseling Mary and Bob," Deacon LaPree told her.

"That could take a while," Roseanna muttered. It was common knowledge that Mary and Bob fought more than anyone in the church, and it always took a lot of time to get them back on speaking terms.

"I'll have to check with Mama," Roseanna said, rejoining the prince.

Mama was talking to Maurice as they walked over to her.

"Let me do the talking," the prince said and handed Mama his card. Then in a voice as smooth as Grandma's freshly churned butter, he continued, "Ma-am, I'm J.T. Prince. I need to talk to Roseanna. Is it okay if she has lunch with me in town? I know you would never allow your daughter to go off alone with a stranger so is there someone who could go with us?"

"Belle could go, Mama," Roseanna suggested.

"I don't know," Mama said hesitantly.

"Please," Roseanna pleaded.

"We'll take good care of them, Ma-am," Maurice promised.

"I guess it will be all right," Mama said.

"Thanks, Mama ," Roseanna exclaimed, hugging her and running off to find Belle.

"Thank you, " the prince said, shaking Mama's hand. "We'll have them back safe and sound in a couple of hours."

Roseanna felt like a princess as she sat next to Belle in the limousine. 'The Prince' as they called him sat facing them.

"Are you girls enjoying the ride?" he asked.

"Yes sir, very much," they answered.

"This car sure goes fast," Belle commented.

The prince laughed. "I guess it must seem so to you, but Maurice seldom exceeds the speed limit."

Roseanna's thoughts went back to the day she rode down this highway with Brad in Earl's bumpy old truck and all the fun they'd had. A shadow passed over her heart. She wished Brad were here.

"Looks like we're coming into town," the prince said. "Do you know a good place to eat?"

"Do you want fancy big city food?" Roseanna asked.

"Or burgers and fries?" Belle blurted out.

Roseanna elbowed her in the side.

"Burgers and fries, of course," the prince said, laughing and winking at Roseanna.

Belle blushed. She hadn't meant to be so obvious.

Ed's Drive In bustled with activity. Adults sat around the tables and in the booths, laughing and visiting; small children romped on the playground; noisy teenagers congregated for a Sunday afternoon of fun. Horns beeped; kids yelled.

"Looks like the neighborhood hang-out, " the prince scowled. "We can't talk here. Why don't we get our food to go, and eat in the car."

The girls nodded eagerly, happy for any excuse to spend more time in the limousine.

The prince took their orders and stepped up to the counter. "We'll have four super-size burgers with everything, four large orders of fries, and four of the biggest chocolate milkshakes you have."

"That will be $22.10," the pretty young waitress said, ringing up the order.

"Keep the change, little darlin'," he said, handing her a hundred dollar bill.

"Thank you, sir!" she exclaimed, her eyes wide with wonder.

"I'll get right to the point," the prince told Roseanna as they got in the car and sat back to enjoy their meal. "You remember Robert Scott, the man who was here a few weeks ago?"

Roseanna nodded. "He ran out of gas over on the highway."

"Yeah, that's him. He works for me, and he told me about you. I came all the way from Nashville just to hear you sing. I like what I heard."

"Thank you," Roseanna said, "but I don't understand what this is all about."

"It's about the chance of a lifetime for you darlin'. I own a recording studio in Nashville, and I want to record some of your songs. With your talent and my know-how, you'll be a star in no time. I guarantee it."

Roseanna sat there in a daze. "Is this for real?" she asked.

"As real as the limo you're riding in," he assured her. "Come away with me, baby, on back to Nashville and I'll make all your dreams come true. You can have it all: money, fame, diamonds, cars. Anything you want can be yours."

Roseanna's dreams flashed before her eyes, Could they really come true? Were they within her grasp? Did she only have to reach out and grab hold of them, or was this just another fantasy?

"I must have your answer now," the prince said. "I've got pressing business in Nashville tomorrow, so I must leave shortly."

Roseanna's head was spinning. She couldn't think straight. "Belle, help me," she pleaded.

"Sorry, sis, this is your call," Belle said gently.

"You know how much I've always dreamed of this, how much I want it."

"More than you want to marry Brad?" Belle asked softly.

"I love Brad dearly, and someday I will marry him, but I can't pass up this chance for the life I've always dreamed of. Brad will understand; I know he will. The answer is yes, Mr. Prince, I will go with you."

"Look out Nashville," he whooped, "Country Music's gonna have a new Queen!"

It wasn't easy to persuade Mama to let Roseanna go. The prince with all his smooth talk couldn't do it. He was about to give up when Maurice intervened.

"Sister LeBlanc," he said "I'll watch over Miss Roseanna and take care of her as if she were my own. I won't let anything happen to your little girl. I give you my word as a Christian."

"Well, if you promise to take care of her, I guess it will be okay," Mama said. "I give my permission for her to go."

"Since Roseanna is under-age, you'll need to sign these contracts along with her," the prince told Mama, taking a pen from his pocket and writing with his left hand.

Grandma gasped. "He's left-handed! You know what that means."

"Grandma, that's just another one of your superstitions," Roseanna chided.

"No, I've seen it with my own eyes," she affirmed. "All left-handed people have magical powers; that's why Treaters are left-handed so they can use their magic to heal folks."

"Treaters are Cajun folk-medicine practitioners," Roseanna explained to the prince.

"That's right, and they possess magical powers along with all other left-handed people," Grandma snorted, shaking her finger in his face. "Don't you go using your magic on our Roseanna or you'll answer to me."

"Yes ma-am," he said amusingly.

"It's getting late," Maurice said, pointing to his watch.

"Yeah, we're all finished here and we've got to be going. We'll see you on Tuesday, Roseanna," he said handing her a plane ticket. "I brought it hoping you'd say yes."

"I don't know," Mama said nervously. "Roseanna's never been on a plane…"

The prince broke in before Mama had a chance to change her mind. "It's non-stop from New Orleans to Nashville, and Maurice will be waiting at the airport. She'll be perfectly safe, I assure you."

"I guess it's up to you, Roseanna," Mama said looking at her.

Roseanna nodded eagerly.

"I've got to tell Brad," she said excitedly as soon as the big white limousine drove away. She ran the short distance to the church and knocked on the door of the parsonage.

"Hey, sweetheart," Brad said opening the door. He took her in his arms and kissed her. "Sorry I missed you after church this morning. Why didn't you wait?"

"You were busy with Mary and Bob, and Mr. Prince was in a hurry."

"That flashy fellow in the big car," Brad said. "What does he have to do with anything?"

"That's what I want to tell you," she exclaimed. "He came all the way from Nashville just to hear me sing!"

"How did he know about you?"

"Robert Scott, the man who was here a few weeks ago works for him, and he told him about me."

"I still don't understand," Brad mumbled.

"Mr. Prince owns a recording studio, and he wants me to go to Nashville and record some of my songs."

51

"Wow! That's great! I knew my girl had talent," Brad boasted, "After coming all that distance, I suppose he had a few choice words to say when you turned him down."

"I-I didn't turn him down, I'm going. I have my plane ticket right here. I leave Tuesday."

The color drained from Brad's face. "But why?" he stammered.

"This is what I've dreamed of all my life, Brad, a chance to taste life outside the bayou."

"What about our dreams?" His voice trembled. "What about the wedding?"

"The weddings not off, just postponed. I love you Bradley Lefourche and I want to be your wife. Nothing on earth can change that."

"You think that now, but if you go to Nashville with that man, everything will change. I don't trust him, Roseanna. He'll end up hurting you."

"He's interested in my talent, not me, and besides he's been a real gentleman."

"My sweet, trusting Roseanna. You've never been out in the world. You don't know what it's like out there," he warned her. "There's all kinds of snares just waiting for a young girl like you."

"I'll be careful, Brad, don't worry."

He shook his head, "I am worried, sweetheart. That man with his smooth talk and tall promises; the lure of the big city lights; my heart tells me if you go, you won't be back."

"I'll always come back to you. Besides, I may not be good enough to make it in Nashville."

"You're good enough," he muttered.

"Even if I do make it big, that won't change my feelings for you. I'll always love you and I will be back. Please promise you'll wait for me."

"No, I won't wait!" Brad exclaimed emphatically. "I'm coming with you! I can preach in Nashville same as here."

Roseanna winced as tears filled her eyes. Dear, sweet Brad. His love for her was so pure, so unselfish. Why couldn't she be like him? She wished she could forget this dream of hers and stay here with him, but she couldn't. Neither could she let him make this sacrifice.

"It would be wonderful having you with me in Nashville, but I can't let you do it, Brad," she said tearfully. "You told me yourself that this is where you belong. Your commitment and calling is here, helping these people. If you give that up, you'll be giving up a big part of yourself. I can't let you do that."

"Then stay here with me," he pleaded.

"Please try to understand, Brad. I want to stay here but there's this yearning deep inside me that won't let me..."

"Don't ask me to understand," he snapped angrily. "I'll never understand why our love is not enough for you."

"Please don't be mad at me," she cried. "Please don't stop loving me."

"I could sooner stop breathing than to stop loving you." He took her in his arms and held her close. "Let's not spend our last hours together fighting," he said gently, wiping the tears from her eyes.

She nodded. They made a truce not to dwell on her leaving until it was time for her to go.

Tuesday came all too quickly. Roseanna's heart was breaking as she said a tearful goodbye to Mama, the girls and Grandma. They had never seemed more precious. She clung to Belle. How could she say good-by to her? Belle was more than her sister; she was her confidante, her best friend.

"Oh Belle, I'll miss you most of all," she whispered, holding on to her tightly.

"Go on, get out of here before you miss your plane and we have to say these good-byes all over again," Belle cried, tears streaming down her face.

The family followed Roseanna and Brad out to his car and waved until they were out of sight.

"What's wrong with me, Brad?" Roseanna sobbed, not able to stop the tears. "Why can't I be happy just to stay here with the people I love most in the world? Why do I have to leave and make everyone sad? Am I some kind of monster?"

"Come here," he said putting his arm around her and pulling her close.

It felt good having him hold her. She snuggled closer and laid her head on his shoulder.

"I'd like to stay here like this forever," she whispered.

"No one's making you leave," he said with a touch of anger in his voice, then softly he added, "I just want you to be happy, sweetheart."

"I know," she said, kissing him on the cheek.

They didn't say much the rest of the trip. Small talk seemed inappropriate, and it was too painful talking about the things they really felt.

They barely reached the airport in time for Roseanna to get checked in before her flight number was called.

"I guess this is it," she mumbled, her voice cracking.

"No, I won't let you go," Brad said, pulling her into his arms and kissing her. All the love in his heart was in that kiss.

The sweetness of his kiss consumed her. She wanted to stay in his arms forever. She hated the longing inside her that was pulling her away from him. Like a giant magnet, it was drawing her to the bright lights and glitter of the world outside the bayou with a force so strong she was powerless to stop it.

They were both in tears as the last boarding call was given.

"Don't go, Roseanna," he said, his eyes looking pleadingly into hers.

"I've *got* to go," she cried, and pulling away from him, she half-ran, half-stumbled into the portable corridor that led to the airplane.

Tears ran unbridled down Brad's face as he watched the big jet-liner taxi down the runway and lift swiftly into the air, disappearing into the clouds, taking his beloved Roseanna away from him. Perhaps forever.

Chapter 6

Roseanna opened her eyes. "Belle," she whispered, reaching over to wake her sister. The bed was empty beside her. She sat up and looked around. This wasn't her room. Where was she?

"Nashville," she mumbled. Questions flooded her mind. Whose bed was she in and how did she get there? What happened here?

Roseanna shook her head to clear out the cobwebs. She remembered the brightly lit runway as the plane landed in Nashville—Maurice was there waiting and drove her to the prince's apartment—there was a party—people everywhere—and—and—nothing. The rest of last night was a complete blank. An uneasy feeling gripped her. Was Brad right about the prince? Was Grandma?

She jumped out of bed and ran out of the room looking for someone to answer her questions. Maurice was in the kitchen.

"Miss Roseanna, you're awake," he said.

"What happened last night?" she blurted out. "I don't remember."

"All I know is that after the party we found you asleep in J.T.'s bed. We didn't have the heart to wake you, so he slept on the couch."

A simple explanation Roseanna thought, chiding herself for her suspicious mind. "I'm not used to such late hours," she said sheepishly.

"We'd better get some food in you," Maurice said. "You must be starving."

"I can't eat a bite—I feel sick. Coming here was a mistake—leaving Brad was a mistake. I want to go home—I want Brad. Please take me home, Maurice," she cried as thoughts of home overwhelmed her.

Maurice put his arms around her. "Don't cry, child, it will be all right," he said compassionately.

" My family and Brad, I miss them so much. He pleaded with me not to leave him—why did I do it? If I could take it back, I'd never get on that plane, I wouldn't leave them." Sobs racked her body.

"There, there, Miss Roseanna," Maurice said. "What you've got is a bad case of homesickness; that's the worst sickness there is, cause it's a sickness of the heart and it hurts real bad, but it will get better, I promise. Now, run wash your face while I whip up a batch of my blueberry pancakes. Topped with my special blueberry syrup, they're guaranteed to cure even the worst case of homesickness. I promised your mother I'd take good care of you, and that includes making sure you eat right. Now scoot."

An aroma of blueberries filled the air as Roseanna walked back into the kitchen. It smelled good, maybe she could eat after all.

"I set up a table out on the balcony," Maurice said, picking up a large tray loaded with stacks of buttered pancakes, a mug of warm blueberry syrup and a big pot of coffee.

"Wow! I've never seen anything like this," Roseanna exclaimed walking out on the balcony. "Look at those tall buildings! My first real glimpse of Nashville, and what a view!"

"Wait til you see the rest of it," Maurice said laughing,

"Is Mr. Prince eating with us?" she asked.

"No, he left early for a meeting down town. He's going to meet us later."

"These are good," she said, hungrily devouring the pancakes Maurice piled on her plate. "I didn't know I was so hungry."

"Did I get the coffee too strong for you?" he asked.

Roseanna laughed. "You've never tasted our coffee back home, have you? This is mild compared to it."

He smiled. "It's good to hear you laugh, Miss Roseanna."

"You were right. Your pancakes did the trick," she told him. "I'm feeling much better. Don't tell Mr Prince that I wanted to go home, okay?"

"It's our little secret," Maurice promised as he piled more pancakes on their plates and refilled their coffee cups.

"I'll do the dishes," Roseanna offered when they finished eating.

"We don't do dishes," he explained, "we put them in the dishwasher."

"You mean I don't have to wash dishes?"

"Never again," he replied laughingly.

"Nashville's sounding better all the time," she exclaimed, grinning from ear to ear.

"Run along and get dressed while I clear the table. We're meeting J.T. in a little while. He's got a surprise for you."

"What kind of surprise?" she asked eagerly.

"It's a secret," he said. "Now hurry. We don't want to keep him waiting."

Roseanna gazed in wonder as they rode through the streets of Nashville. "Why are we stopping here?" she asked as Maurice parked the limousine in front of Milady's Dress Shoppe.

"J.T. is already here," he said gesturing towards a small red sports car. "Go on in, he'll explain everything."

"Ritzy," she muttered as she walked into the shop. Exquisite sequined gowns fashioned on life-like mannequins were everywhere. Their beauty took her breath. "I don't belong here," she whispered, and turned to run out the door.

"Over here," a voice called softly.

The prince was sitting on a gold brocaded settee. A nearby table, covered with a gold-trimmed white satin tablecloth, held a large silver coffee urn. Silver trays were filled with goodies of all kinds.

The prince was sipping coffee from a small fancy cup. Roseanna sat down beside him.

"I hate these tiny cups," he grumbled. "Let's hurry and get this over with so I can get a real cup of coffee."

"What are we doing here?" she whispered.

"Didn't Maurice tell you? You're getting a new wardrobe."

Roseanna panicked. "I can't afford these things. I have some money but not near enough for clothes like this."

"Relax, baby, I'm paying."

"No, you're not! I can't accept gifts like this from you." She was almost in tears.

"This is not a gift," he assured her, "This is business; these clothes will be written off on my expense account. Believe me, baby, when your records start rolling I'll get my money back in no time. Now let's get this show on the road." He motioned to a young woman standing nearby.

"Mavis, we're ready" he said. "This is Roseanna. See what you can do for her."

"She's a natural beauty," the woman said looking Roseanna over. "Don't worry, J.T., it'll be easy dressing her."

Roseanna wondered why Mavis was working here as a saleslady. Tall and graceful, she looked more like a model or a ballerina. Flaxen curls framed a perfectly flawless face. Her peaches-and-cream complexion and blue-green eyes were highlighted by the soft aqua blouse she wore. Roseanna felt drab standing next to her.

Mavis took Roseanna to a lavish dressing room with a settee like the ones outside and a dressing table which held cosmetics of all kinds.

"Hmm, what size are you?" Mavis pondered out loud.

"Mama buys a size six pattern," Roseanna said, then blushed realizing that was not the right thing to say.

"That's a starting point," Mavis said kindly. "Don't worry, dear, if you find something you like, we'll make it fit. Now make yourself comfortable and I'll be back shortly."

Roseanna felt like a fish out of water. What was she doing in a place like this? Home seemed so far away.

Mavis returned with an armload of beautiful gowns in several colors.

"Sit down," she said, motioning to the dressing table. "Just a touch of blush," she continued, gently stroking the small brush along Roseanna's cheekbones. "Not all of J.T.'s girls are as pretty as you."

Roseanna flinched. "I'm not his girl," she retorted. "He's recording some of my songs, that's all. I'm engaged to a wonderful man and as soon as my business is finished here, I'm going back home and marry him."

"I see," Mavis said, a bit skeptically. "I wish you the best. Now let's try this white gown first."

Roseanna slipped into the gown. It fit like a glove. Mavis stopped her before she could look in the mirror.

"You need this," she said, brushing Roseanna's hair gently away from her face and securing it loosely with a diamond studded headband. "Now you can look."

Roseanna looked in the mirror and gasped. That beautiful creature reflected there couldn't possibly be her. "Oh, my," she said breathlessly, "I feel just like Cinderella."

"Your Prince Charming awaits," Mavis said, gesturing towards the prince.

"Do I have to go out there?" Roseanna asked, touching her bare shoulders. "I've never worn a dress like this before."

"Don't be silly; you look beautiful," Mavis said nudging her out the door.

Shyly, Roseanna walked over to the prince.

He let out a whistle. "Wowie, baby! You look amazing! We'll take that one, Mavis."

Roseanna modeled dress after dress. She soon forgot her shyness and got into the spirit of it. She twirled and turned and posed with each new dress. She came out dressed in a lovely red gown sparkling with sequins; the prince grabbed her and like two kids they went waltzing across the floor, dancing cheek to cheek, to imaginary music. They laughed so hard tears rolled down their faces. Everyone stopped to watch. Mavis cleared her throat.

Regaining his composure the prince said, "I think we've seen enough. Along with the white one, we'll take this one, the blue-green one and the bright pink one. We'll also need shoes to match each gown and an evening bag, and that thing-ama-jig in her hair."

Mavis laughed. "I'll get everything together and send them over in a couple of days."

"She's too pretty to be working as a saleslady. She should be modeling the clothes instead of selling them," Roseanna remarked when they got out of earshot of Mavis.

"Mavis doesn't just work here, she owns the shop. She also designs most of the gowns. Do you think I would trust your wardrobe to just anyone?" the prince said as they walked to the limousine.

Maurice opened the door for them.

"I can't wait to show you all the beautiful things I got today," she told him as she got into the car.

"That's just the beginning," the prince said. "We've got a few more stops to make before your wardrobe is complete. I'll leave my car here and pick it up later."

Their next stop was a Western-Wear store. The prince picked out matching black and white outfits for Roseanna and himself and boots for her.

"I can't wear this," she cried, walking out of the dressing room in a black leather jacket and matching mini-skirt.

"Trust me, baby, I know what's best for you. It's the latest fad and looks great on you. We'll take it," he told the clerk.

A few more stops, and the limo was loaded down with boxes and bags of designer jeans (two sizes too small), skirts, blouses, shoes, and all the trimmings.

"All that shopping made me hungry," the prince said. "Let's eat before we go home. I know this all-you-can-eat- pizza place where they serve the best pizza in town."

After they had eaten their fill of pizza, they decided to take Roseanna on a tour of the city.

"This is a dream come true," she exclaimed as they rode through brightly lit streets. "Today has been one of the best days of my life. I want to thank you for everything, Mr. Prince."

"Stick with me, baby; this is just the beginning of happy days. Tomorrow, I'll take you over to my studio and introduce you around and we'll start making plans to record your songs."

Roseanna sighed happily. Her dreams were really coming true.

"I'll sleep on the couch tonight," she offered when they got home around midnight.

"I won't hear of it," the prince said. "We have extra rooms here. Tomorrow we'll turn them into a wing for you, but tonight you will sleep in my room and I'll sleep out here."

Roseanna was too tired to argue. She quickly changed into a pink cotton nightgown and fell into bed totally exhausted.

In the quiet of the darkness her thoughts turned home. "Brad. I need to write Brad," she mumbled, but she couldn't drag herself out of bed. "I'll do it tomorrow," she vowed, yawning and drifting off to sleep.

Chapter 7

"Happy birthday," Maurice greeted Roseanna as she walked in the kitchen. He handed her a cup of coffee.

"Thanks, Maurice," she said sitting down at the breakfast nook. "My eighteenth birthday; it's hard to believe I'm spending it in Nashville."

"Are you happy, Miss Roseanna," he asked with concern in his voice.

"Mostly I am," she said. "I'm sorry about postponing my wedding but I'm not sorry about coming to Nashville, so many wonderful things have happened to me these past two months."

"How's your albums coming along?"

"I've finished my part finally," she replied. "I never dreamed recording songs was so complicated. I thought I'd get up there, sing into a microphone and that would be it. I didn't know about all that technical stuff. I never would have made it without Mr. Prince."

"J.T. has a head for business all right," Maurice said proudly. "His studio is one of the most successful in Nashville. He has a knack for making money."

"Sounds like you know him pretty well," she said.

"We go way back," Maurice told her. "I've worked for his family since he was a small boy. I met his father during the worst time of my life. My wife and daughter were killed by a drunk driver when my little girl was five years old..."

"I'm so sorry," Roseanna gasped.

"All the feelings inside me died along with them," he continued with tears in his eyes. "I bummed around the country for a couple of years not caring what happened to me. That's when his father came along. He helped me turn my life around and offered me a job. J.T. was about five years old at the time, and taking care of him helped me deal with loss of my own child. His parents were killed when he was fifteen, and I stayed on to take care of him. When he moved to Nashville, he insisted I come along. I tried calling him Mr. Prince when we got here, but he wouldn't hear of it, saying I was the closest thing to family that he had left."

Just then the doorbell rang. It was the apartment manager.

"Mr. Prince asked me to hand-deliver this," he said handing Roseanna a large white envelope. "This package came for you, too."

"It's from Brad!" she squealed with delight, tearing open the package. A gold locket was inside along with a note. She read it eagerly.

Happy birthday sweetheart,

I was going to give this to you on our wedding day but I want you to have it for your birthday. It belonged to my grandmother. She passed it down to me to give to that special girl when I found her. Roseanna, you will always be that one and only 'special girl' for me. Wear the locket and think of me until we can be together again.

Forever yours,

Brad

"It's so beautiful! I'll never take it off!" she exclaimed, fastening the locket around her neck.

Maurice cleared his throat and pointed to the envelope.

"Oh, yeah," Roseanna muttered opening it. A hand-written invitation was inside.

Roseanna,

Please have dinner with me tonight to celebrate your birthday. I have a special evening planned. Wear the white gown. I'll pick you up at eight.

J.T. Prince

"Wow," Roseanna sighed, "two great surprises in one day; first the locket, and now this. Do you know where we're going, Maurice?"

"No, but it will be some place elegant. J.T. never does anything half-way."

"I've never been to a fancy restaurant. I won't know how to act," Roseanna fretted.

"Just be yourself and everything will turn out fine," he assured her.

"I wish I was as certain of that as you are," she said finishing a bowl of cornflakes and gulping down a glass of orange juice.

More coffee?" he asked.

"Yes, I'll drink it in my room," she answered. "I need to start getting ready for tonight."

Maurice laughed heartily. "You only have twelve hours," he teased.

"It takes some of us longer," she laughingly yelled back as she scurried to her quarters.

She sat amid plump throw pillows on the over-stuffed couch in her sitting room writing to Brad, thanking him for the locket; telling him she would cherish it always, and that it was the most perfect gift he could have given her. Tears fell on the pages as she wrote of her love for him and the hope she had of being home soon so they could begin their life together. She didn't tell him about the invitation from the prince or of their dinner date tonight.

Thoughts of dining in a fancy restaurant sent butterflies fluttering in her stomach. Memories of another dinner long ago flashed through her mind. It was at Reverend Trosclair's house and she was just a girl. She could see it now; there was a big pickle on her plate and wanting to be proper, she tried cutting it with a fork. The fork became a launching pad and sent the pickle flying through the air until it landed, ker-plunk, right in Mrs Trosclair's plate. The minister and his wife had a good laugh, but Roseanna felt stupid and clumsy.

"I'll mess up tonight; I know I will. I just won't go," she exclaimed. But she would, the excitement of it over-rode any qualms she might have.

She searched through every book of etiquette in the prince's library hoping for a crash course in proper manners, but at the end of the day she still wasn't sure of herself.

She took a leisurely bubble-bath, then added a touch of blush to her cheeks. She wanted to look perfect tonight, like the day she first modeled the gown. She brushed her hair back gently and secured it with the diamond headband. She slipped into the white gown and looked in the mirror.

A slight frown crossed her face. Her bare shoulders bothered her. What would Mama think? She pressed the gold locket to her heart. Brad certainly wouldn't approve, but the prince had requested that she wear this gown.

A soft knock at the door interrupted her thoughts. He was here. After a quick glance in the mirror, she opened the door.

Standing there in a black tuxedo, he indeed looked like a prince: regal and majestic. The sight of him took Roseanna's breath away.

"Wheet-Wheel!" he whistled. "You're drop-dead gorgeous!"

"Thank you," she mumbled softly. "You're not so bad, yourself."

"I haven't seen that locket before," he mentioned as they walked into the foyer.

"Brad sent it for my birthday."

"It's lovely," he said, "but this will look better with your gown. Happy birthday, Roseanna." He handed her a small box.

She stared at the diamond necklace inside. "I-I can't accept this, it's too much."

"Nonsense. Every girl deserves something special for her eighteenth birthday." He took the locket from around her neck, and replaced it with the necklace. "There, that's better," he said, turning her around to face the mirror. "See?"

She nodded, awed by the beauty of the necklace.

"There's a nip in the air tonight, I think you might need this." He took a white mink stole from the closet and placed it around her shoulders. "Your carriage awaits, My Lady," he said. He bowed, took her arm, and escorted her to the limousine.

Roseanna truly felt like royalty.

"Welcome, Mr Prince," the lovely young hostess said when they entered the restaurant. "Everything's ready just as you requested. Follow me, please."

Heads turned as Roseanna walked through the restaurant on the arm of the prince. Comments drifted through the air.

"What a striking couple."

"She's so beautiful."

"I wonder who she is?"

The prince, hearing the last comment, stopped dead in his tracks.

"Wait a minute, darlin'," he told the hostess. "Folks, I'm J.T. Prince," he announced. "You've probably heard of me."

They nodded.

"I'd like for you to meet Roseanna, my newest recording artist and soon-to-be the new queen of country music. Watch for her albums, they're coming out any day now."

A cheer went up from around the room.

Roseanna, blushing and smiling, waved to the crowd.

"I'm not used to this," she whispered to the prince.

"Get used to it baby. Before too long, Roseanna will be a household name in all the homes across these United States," he said as the hostess opened the door to the private dining room.

"Enjoy your evening," she said motioning them inside.

Roseanna gazed in wonder. Tall white tapers, glowing in brass candelabras, furnished the only light in the room. Fragrance from fresh cut flowers filled the air. A candlelit table covered with white satin and lace was set for two.

"Our dinner is ready," the prince said. "I took the liberty of ordering ahead. I hope you don't mind."

"Of course not," she replied.

"The food here is some of the finest in Nashville," he remarked as the waiter served their salads.

Roseanna watched the prince pick up his salad fork and begin to eat, then she did the same. Later, when the main course was served, she again followed his lead.

"This is wonderful!" she exclaimed, taking a bite of the food on her plate.

"Prime rib is their specialty," he told her. "I'm glad you like it."

By the time dessert was served, Roseanna felt much more relaxed.

"Chocolate mousse for the lady," the waiter said, setting the delicacy before her.

"Irish coffee for the gentleman. Will there anything else, sir?"

"No, thank you. Make sure we're not disturbed for the rest of the evening," the prince said as the waiter left the room.

Roseanna had stars in her eyes. She had never been treated with such renown.

"Now that we're alone, I've got a surprise for you; something big, baby," he told her, reaching for a bottle of champagne. He started to pour some in her glass.

She stopped him. "I don't want any of that," she said emphatically.

"You're eighteen now and it's only champagne," he said, "One little glass won't hurt you and besides, what we're celebrating tonight calls for champagne."

"What is it?" she asked eagerly.

"A wonderful surprise, darlin'. I'll tell you later, but first the champagne."

Roseanna took a sip, then another one. It wasn't so bad. Soon her glass was empty. The prince refilled it; soon the bottle was empty.

"Now let's dance," he said, pulling her to her feet. He pushed a button and soft music filled the room. He held her close while they danced, which was fine with Roseanna, cause she was feeling light-headed and giddy.

"Thank you for making this my best birthday ever, Mr. Prince"

"For-crying-out-loud, Roseanna, stop calling me *Mr.* Prince. I'm not *that* old. I'm only thirty-two. Call me J.T.

"Oh, I could never call you J.T.," she said frivolously. "I could call you prince; that's what you are, you know—Prince Charming. Belle and me named you that the first time we saw you."

He laughed. "Prince it is, and I'm going to hold you to that even though tomorrow you probably won't remember saying it."

Roseanna snuggled closer to him. She clasped her arms around his neck and looked into his eyes. Dark, moody and black as midnight, those eyes pierced into her very soul and held her captive, pulling her into the turbulence reflected in them. She trembled.

The prince kissed her in a way she'd never been kissed before. Emotions raged inside her that she never knew existed. She kissed him back passionately.

Somewhere, deep in the recesses of her mind, thoughts of Brad surfaced, but they were pushed aside by the feelings that swallowed her up as she clung to the prince. She kissed him again.

Suddenly, he pulled away. "Roseanna, I'm sorry, I shouldn't have kissed you like that. Please forgive me."

"Don't apologize, kiss me again," she said, putting her arms around him, pulling him close and kissing him over and over. "Don't stop, I want you..."

"No, that's the champagne talking," he said, pushing her away gently. "I'm sorry, I didn't know it would hit you that hard."

He wanted nothing more than to take her in his arms and make love to her, but tonight wasn't the time; she'd had too much to drink. If he let things go too far, it would send her scurrying back home, right into the arms of her preacher. He could wait.

"Come sit down and I'll tell you my surprise," he said, leading her over to the table. "What I said before, out in the restaurant, about your albums is true; they're being released in a couple of days."

"For real?" she asked, her voice fuzzy.

"Yeah, baby, by this time next week you'll be on the airways in all the major cities."

"That's wonderful," she lisped. "It's a dream come true."

"Stick with me, darlin' and all your dreams will come true," he said lightly, but his thoughts were troubled.

How would Roseanna feel tomorrow when the champagne wore off. What if she wanted to go home and marry her preacher—that would ruin all of his plans. He decided to sweeten the deal with an offer he felt certain she couldn't resist.

"That's only half of my surprise," he told her. "I've made arrangements for you to sing at the Grand Ole Opry."

"Me, sing at the Opry? I've always wanted to do that."

"It means you'll have to stay here in Nashville a while longer."

"Of course I'll stay," she said loudly. "I'll write a song 'specially for the Opry. I'll even..."

"Slow down, darlin'," he said, laughing. "There's plenty of time for that. I think we'd better get you home now."

On the ride home Roseanna fell asleep in the limousine. The prince nudged her, making sure she was fast asleep, then dialed the phone.

"Robert," he said in a hushed voice, "J.T. here. Call Logan Ames and tell him I need a favor."

"The man from the Grand Ole Opry?"

"Yeah. Tell him I need Roseanna to sing at the Opry this month."

"That's short notice."

"Yeah, but he can handle it. He owes me big time and I'm calling in the debt."

"I'll try."

"Don't try. Do it," the prince said gruffly. "My future with Roseanna depends on it." Not bothering to explain, he hung up.

"I will have a future with you, baby," he said, stroking her hair. "I couldn't take advantage of you tonight, but someday I will have you. I'll make you forget that preacher fellow and then you'll be mine, only mine, forever."

Chapter 8

"Let me in, Roseanna," the prince called softly, tapping gently on the door.

"Go away, please."

"No, I won't go away. We've got to talk—about last night."

"No," she cried, "I can't."

"I've got to talk to you, Roseanna. Open the door, please."

"Just go away," she pleaded tearfully.

"I'm not leaving," he said firmly. "I could get the key from Maurice."

"No!" she cried desperately, " he must never know." Reluctantly, she opened the door.

"Roseanna, I'm sorry about last night," the prince said, walking into the room.

She turned away from him.

"Look at me, please."

"No, I-I can't. I'm too ashamed," she sobbed.

He put his hands gently on her shoulders and turned her around. "Roseanna, listen to me. What happened last night was not your fault. I'm to blame."

"It *was* my fault," she cried. "I wanted you to hold me in your arms and kiss me like that, I didn't want you to stop---I'm just a tramp."

"We only kissed," he said.

"It's more than the kisses—It's the way I felt—the shameful way I acted." She burst into tears again.

"Don't cry, baby, you didn't do anything wrong. The champagne made you crazy and that's my fault. You wouldn't have acted like that without it. I came in here to apologize and beg your forgiveness."

"You don't think I'm cheap and trashy?"

"Believe me, baby, I've been around. I know cheap and trashy. If you were that kind of girl, last night would not have ended with just a kiss."

"But what about Brad? I cheated on him."

"I don't think kissing adds up to cheating," he told her.

"In my heart I cheated on him and that's just as bad," she said. "How do I explain last night to him?"

"Don't try darlin'. Telling him would be a big mistake. It would only hurt him, and for what? Last night didn't change your feelings for him, did it?"

"Of course not," she cried a bit defensively. "I love him with all my heart."

"Okay, trust me on this, baby. What he don't know won't hurt him."

"But what if he finds out?"

"Who's gonna tell him? We're the only ones who know, and we'll keep it our little secret."

"Thanks for understanding, Mr. Prince."

"Roseanna, you promised, no more *Mr.* Prince."

She blushed, remembering the promise. "Thank you, *Prince.*"

"That's my girl. Now run wash your face, and let's see what Maurice has for breakfast."

She nodded and headed for the bathroom.

80

"Whew, that was close," the prince muttered, "but I pulled it off. Roseanna's gullible. I can handle her but if that preacher ever finds out about last night, he'll come straight to Nashville and take her back home and marry her as soon as possible." He clenched his fist. "Over my dead body!" he declared hostilely.

"Did you say something?" Roseanna asked, walking back into the room.

"Just thinking out loud, darlin'."

"What's wrong, Miss Roseanna?" Maurice asked later as they sat around the breakfast nook. "You're not eating."

"I'm not hungry, Maurice," she replied in a subdued voice.

"Big night, huh?"

" A fabulous night," the prince spoke up before she had a chance to answer. "Roseanna was the envy of every woman in the place."

"I don't wonder, the way she looked last night," Maurice said proudly.

"Thank you both," she said, forcing a smile.

"Roseanna, tell him the great news," the prince suggested excitedly.

"My albums are coming out this week and I'm singing at the Grand Ole Opry," she said with a bit more enthusiasm.

"That is great news! I'm so proud of you," Maurice exclaimed, giving her a hug.

"Thanks, Maurice. Now, if you'll both excuse me, I'm going to my room."

"She's not herself today," Maurice remarked after she left . "Did something happen last night?" He eyed the prince suspiciously.

"Not that I know of. I guess she's just drained from the excitement of it all."

"I hope that's all it is," Maurice said still eyeing him.

"I've got a plan that will cheer her up," the prince said, rushing out the door.

Roseanna hurried to her room and fell across the bed, clutching Brad's locket in her hand. She fastened it around her neck. "I'll never take it off again, Brad," she whispered, tears flowing down her face.

Her thoughts were muddled. Why did last night bother her so? It only happened because of the champagne; it didn't mean anything.

"Brad's the man I love. I want to be in his arms and feel the sweetness of his kiss, the safeness of his love." She trembled. "Oh, Brad, I need you here now, I need your strength. When I think of how close I came to betraying our love.." she put her head down on her pillow and wept bitterly. Haunted by the memory of last night, she closed her eyes, trying to erase the scenes from her mind.

A knock at the door startled her.

"Miss Roseanna, I have a tray for you," Maurice called softly. "Please let me in."

She jumped up quickly and opened the door. "Is it lunch time already?" she asked, rubbing her eyes. "I must have fallen asleep."

"Child, it's two o'clock," he said. "I waited for you to come out to lunch, when you didn't, I brought lunch to you. Are you all right? Did something happen last night?"

"No!" she cried a bit too quickly. Roseanna didn't lie well; she felt sure Maurice saw straight through it. She had to tell another lie to cover it before he asked more questions. "I'm just exhausted from the long hours and late nights I've been keeping. Don't worry about me, Maurice, I'll be fine."

"I'm gonna make sure of that," he said. "Now eat."

"Thanks, I am hungry," she said, devouring the turkey sandwich and fresh vegetables on the tray.

"Knock, knock. Is this a private party or may I join in?" the prince asked walking into the room. "Roseanna, I have something that's gonna cheer you up." He handed her a CD.

She looked at the cover: ROSEANNA: SONGS FROM THE HEART.

"My songs," she cried jubilantly. "It's for real!"

"Yeah, baby. By this time tomorrow, you can hear yourself on the radio, but let's take a listen right now." He put the CD in the stereo.

Strains of "Were I An Eagle, He'd Be There," flowed smoothly through the room.

They listened in silence.

"We've done it!" the prince shouted as the last song ended. He picked Roseanna up and swung her around. "We're on our way, baby!"

"You made it happen," Roseanna exclaimed, throwing her arms around him. She quickly pulled away.

"We did it together, you and me. We make a great team."

"It's beautiful," Maurice said, wiping tears from his eyes.

"This is just the beginning," the prince told them. "Next stop, the Grand Ole Opry! It's all set, baby, you sing there in three weeks."

"Wow! All my dreams are coming true. Thank you, Prince," she said gratefully. "Now, scoot out of here, both of you, I've got a song to write."

"You sure cheered her up," Maurice remarked as they left the room. His suspicions about last night were put to rest.

Hours later, Roseanna sat tapping a pencil on the arm of the couch. Her mind was as blank as the sheet of paper before her. Doubts crept in. Could she write a song here in Nashville, or did the inspiration only come when she was at her special place back home on the bayou?

A voice from the past interrupted her thoughts. Belle's words rang over and over in her ears: "Don't give up on your dreams, Roseanna. They will come true—don't give up, they will come true—don't give up."

"That's it," Roseanna whispered. "Thank you, Belle, I can write my song now."

The next couple of days Roseanna worked on the song. She sorted and resorted her thoughts. She rhymed words and strummed melodies on her guitar. She arranged and rearranged words and phrases. Each syllable was carefully planned out. She put the words down on paper; she played the melody and sang the song.

"That's it!" she exclaimed happily, running to tell the prince and Maurice.

"I've done it," she announced smiling. "I've finished the song."

"Sing it for us, baby," the prince said excitedly.

"Okay, I'll practice on you." She sang the song with all the exuberance she felt inside her and took a bow.

They applauded heartily.

"That's some song," the prince said almost reverently.

"It sent goose-bumps up my spine," Maurice added.

"We've got a hit there, darlin'. I'll get the band together and you can start practicing tomorrow. If they do their part half as well as you've done yours, we'll take the Opry by storm."

Practice was grueling. Arlen, the lead guitarist, didn't want to play the song the way Roseanna had written it.

He'd been around for years; she was a newcomer, what did she know, he argued. His attitude was affecting the rest of the band.

"It's no use," Roseanna cried, a few days before the Opry. "We'll never get it right." She ran from the room.

"Okay, fellows," the prince said sternly, walking in on the conversation. "This is Roseanna's song and you will do it her way. I pay you big bucks and you will do as I say. Do I make myself clear?"

"Yes, boss," they said.

"Arlen?"

"Yes, J.T., only---"

"Arlen." He said in a voice of authority.

"Yes, J.T.," Arlen submitted reluctantly.

Roseanna tingled with excitement one minute, and was nervous as a cat the next as the big white limousine rolled down the streets of Nashville taking her closer to the Grand Ole Opry with every hum of the engine. Questions flooded her mind.

Who would be there tonight? Would they like her? Was her song good enough? Did the band have it right? Their last few practices went well, but still..

"A penny for your thoughts," the prince said, interrupting them,

"You don't want to know," she told him. "My stomach is in knots; I'm not sure I can do this."

"Trust me, baby, you're gonna knock-em-dead tonight."

"But I'll be singing alongside some of the greats of country music."

"You can sing with the best of them, darlin'," he said, taking her hand. "You've got a great voice, you've got a great song, and you're a knock-out to look at. What else do you need?"

"A big dose of courage, maybe."

"Maurice, let's show Roseanna the Opryland Hotel before we go in," the prince said as they drove onto the complex grounds.

"Wow," Roseanna sighed breathlessly as they drove by the brightly-lit hotel. She sat speechless, gazing at it's beauty.

"If you think this is something, just wait 'til you see it at Christmas time," the prince told her.

"I'd love to see it," she said dreamily.

"We'll put that on our agenda, I promise, but now we'd better get over to the Opry. We don't want our star being late."

Maurice drove the limousine up to the guard-gate and stopped. He rolled down the window.

"How's it going, Ray?" the prince asked the man at the gate.

"Just fine, Mr. Prince," the guard replied, waving them through.

Maurice parked at the musicians entrance and the prince and Roseanna got out.

"I'll pick you up here after the show," he said. "I'll be sitting in the audience with Mavis, cheering you on."

"Thanks, Maurice," Roseanna said." "It'll help knowing the two of you are out there."

The prince took her arm, and they walked down the long corridor that led to the back of the theater.

"You can freshen up in here, baby." He opened the door to a small dressing room.

Roseanna viewed herself in the mirror and smiled. She liked the way Mavis had outfitted her. She had chosen a bright fuchsia high-waisted gown with spaghetti straps and a long, close-fitting skirt. The simple, elegant lines of the gown enhanced Roseanna's natural beauty. The diamond necklace was her only accessory. Her hair fell loose down her back.

"Mavis sure knows how to put a outfit together," Roseanna said.

"Yeah, she's a classy lady," the prince agreed. "Now let's get backstage. It's almost show time."

"I won't be first, will I?" she asked in panic.

"Relax, you'll sing somewhere in the middle."

Just then a man dressed in western attire dashed by them and ran out on the stage.

"Do you see who that is!" Roseanna whispered excitedly. "He's the greatest singer in the business. I can't follow him."

"Stop fretting Roseanna and enjoy the show."

She stood there, awe-struck, as the entertainer performed. Applause and shouts from the audience broke the spell as he finished his performance and ran off stage.

Travis Houston, the emcee, walked on stage. "Folks," he announced, "we have a special treat coming up next. A young lady all the way from the bayou country of south Louisiana is making her debut tonight, right here on the stage of the Grand Ole Opry. Let's give a big Nashville welcome to Roseanna!"

Roseanna froze. "I can't do it," she gasped.

"I think she's a little shy, folks," the emcee said. "Let's hear it again for Roseanna."

"Get out there," the prince hissed, giving her a shove.

"Well, if the little lady sings half as good as she looks, we're in for a real treat tonight, folks," Travis

Houston said, taking her hand and leading her to the microphone. "It's all yours, honey."

Roseanna stood there, rigid, guitar in hand. She looked over at her band, they nodded. She looked out at the audience; if only she could spot Mavis and Maurice but all she saw was a sea of faces.

"Folks, I'm a little nervous being up here on this stage. This has been a dream of mine all my life; to sing at the Grand Ole Opry, and now that I'm here, I'm scared to death," she said with a sweet smile that melted the hearts of the audience.

"Everyone's scared the first time, little lady," a voice from the crowd yelled, "just sing for us, honey."

That broke the ice. "Thank you, sir," she said. "I'm ready now. I wrote this song especially for tonight. Someone very dear to me once told me never to give up on my dreams; that they would come true someday, and they have. So Belle, this is for you." She nodded to her band, strummed her guitar and started singing:

> *There's a miner out panning for gold on the wild Colorado,*
> *And he's dirty and hungry and tired, all alone every night;*
> *All his friends say he's crazy, he'll never find any treasure out there,*
> *But he keeps digging and searching and dreaming with all of his might.*
>
> *There's a young girl at the controls of a twin-engine airplane,*
> *And she's taxi-ing out on the runway for her first solo flight;*
> *And her daddy thinks he must be crazy for letting his baby do such a wild thing,*

But then she's dreamed of flying all of her life
with all of her might.

There's a young boy whose doctor said, you'll
never walk again, so give up son,
The boy said I know you'll think I'm crazy, doc,
but that just don't sound right;
So he gets up every morning out of that
wheelchair, with a prayer, and he's into his
workout,
Cause he has a dream that he can accomplish the
impossible with all of his might.

It's a matter of dreams and a dream is worth
finding the courage to chase one,
There's no running away, giving up, quitting, even
when you're losing the fight;
It's a matter of praying for strength even when it
appears there won't be none,
Don't give up on your dreams, son, keep dreaming
with all of your might.

"Just listen to what can happen if you don't give
up."

Well, there's a miner up in Denver who they say is
worth near a half-billion dollars these days,
And there's a young woman high above earth on a
space-shuttle flight;
And there's a young man walking the aisle,
unassisted, to his bride and his future today,
Yeah, they all might be a little crazy but they sure
seem to know how to fight.

It's a matter of dreams and a dream is worth
finding the courage to chase one,

*There's no running away, giving up, quitting, even
when you're losing the fight;
It's a matter of praying for strength even when it
appears there won't be none,
Don't give up on your dreams, son, keep
dreaming with all of your might;
Don't give up on your dreams, son, keep dreaming
with all of your might.*

"Just don't ever quit," Roseanna said, finishing
the song and taking a bow.

The theater exploded with applause. Shouts of
"More! More!" rang through the building.

"Take another bow," the prince told her as she
came running over to him.

The crowd was on its feet, clapping and shouting
"Encore! "Encore!" When the noise died down a little,
that same voice from the audience shouted, "Let the
little lady sing her song again."

"Come on back out here," Travis Houston
called, motioning to Roseanna.

She ran back on stage and with all the emotions
inside her, she sang the song even better than before.

Thunderous applause filled the building as the
audience cheered, standing to their feet and wiping
tears from their eyes.

"They liked me!" Roseanna exclaimed, running
into the arms of the prince.

"They loved you, baby," he yelled, pulling her
close and kissing her. She was so happy, she kissed him
back.

Travis Houston waved to silence the crowd.
"Roseanna, you can come back anytime you want to,"
he said. Another cheer went up.

Meanwhile, back home, a smaller but no less enthusiast cheer went up from the happy group gathered around the radio at Grandma's house.

"That's my little girl," Mama said proudly, as tears flooded down her face.

"Her dreams have come true; she sang at the Grand Ole Opry." Grandma added. "Now, she can come home."

"I'll go to Nashville and bring her back myself," Brad said happily. "By this time next week, our Roseanna will be home and we can start making our wedding plans again."

"I wonder," Belle mused silently. An uneasy feeling gripped her heart.

CHAPTER 9

The brisk October wind whistled gustily, chilling the air, but Brad didn't notice. The happy glow from deep inside his heart sent a warmth pulsating through his entire being. Soon he would be holding Roseanna in his arms again; he would kiss her and it would be as if they had never been separated.

The spring in his step was matched only by the sparkle in his eyes as he walked up to the apartment complex.

"Good morning," he greeted the doorman warmly.

"May I see your pass, sir?" the doorman said, blocking the entrance.

"A pass?" Brad asked puzzled. "I'm here to see Roseanna LeBlanc. Do I need a pass for that?"

"Yes sir. If you don't have a pass or your name's not on the list, you don't get in."

"But I came all the way from Louisiana," Brad explained.

"Were you expected?" the doorman asked. "Maybe your name is on the list."

"No, she didn't know I was coming."

"I'm sorry then, but I can't let you in."

"I've got to see Roseanna," Brad said determinedly. "I'm not leaving."

Just then the apartment manager walked up. "Is something wrong here?" he asked.

The doorman explained the situation.

"I'm sorry young man, but our policy here is to protect our tenants. We can't let you in."

"Sir, I'm sorry about your policy, but I've come a long way to see Roseanna and I'm going to see her. I'm Bradley Lefourche, her fiancee."

"You're the one who sent the package on her birthday," the manager said.

"Yes, a gold locket," Brad replied.

"I remember how happy she was when she received it. I know you're someone special to her, so I'm going to bend the rules a little."

"I can go up to her apartment?"

"It wouldn't do any good," the manager told him, "she's not there."

"I've waited three months, I can wait a little bit longer," Brad assured him.

"I'm not supposed to give out this information," the manager said hesitantly. "It won't do any good to wait, she won't be back for a long time. She left yesterday with Mr Prince and Maurice to go on tour."

"Where?" Brad asked dejectedly.

"I can't answer that. Contact his office, they can give you that information. I'm sorry you missed her, son, but that's all I can tell you."

"Thank you for your kindness," Brad muttered, turning to leave.

The miles of highway stretched endlessly before him. He shivered. The glow in his heart that warmed him had faded and he felt the chill of the blustery October day settle upon him. Roseanna was gone. Would it be forever? Tears stung his eyes.

"Why didn't I let her know I was coming? One little phone call—if anything happens to her." He pulled the car over on the shoulder of the road, put his head down on the steering wheel and prayed.

"Father, Roseanna is out there, in a world that's foreign to her. The pain and disappointment I feel is nothing compared to the fear I have that she will be swept into that world with it's glamour and allure. I put her in your Hands, Father, watch over her, don't let her drift so far away that she can't find her way back to us. Take care of her and keep her safe, I pray."

At the same time hundreds of miles away, Roseanna sat silently, gazing at the rich farmland as the limousine sped along the interstate through the boot hills of Missouri. She had a far-away look in her eyes. Thoughts of Brad filled her heart; troubling thoughts; something was wrong; she could feel his pain. A tear slid down her face.

The prince seeing the tear and sensing her mood, reached over and touched her arm. "Earth to Roseanna. Come in," he chanted teasingly.

"Sorry, my mind was someplace else," she mumbled.

He had to tread lightly here. He weighed his words carefully. "You're homesick, aren't you, baby?"

She nodded. "I miss them all so much."

"I know you do, and I'm sorry, but we've got to strike while the iron is hot. After you sang at the Opry, the phone didn't stop ringing; folks wanting to book you for concerts and personal appearances. This is the lifeline of country music, baby, I couldn't turn them down."

"I understand," she said, "and the concert last night in Memphis was fun."

"The fun's just beginning," he proclaimed. "Next stop, St. Louis, then Chicago and on to points beyond—we're on a roll, baby, nothing can stop us now,"

"We're coming into Sikeston," Maurice said, exiting off the Interstate. "There's a restaurant here

94

called Lambert's. I hear it's good. They throw rolls at you."

"And that's good?" the prince asked skeptically.

Roseanna shrugged.

They decided to give it a try.

An hour later they came out of the restaurant, full, satisfied and in a good mood.

"That was some fine eating," the prince said, rubbing his stomach.

"And you only missed 'one throwed roll'," Roseanna teased.

"Not bad for a southpaw," he replied, laughing heartily.

Maurice spoke up. "I liked everything about that place; the relaxed down home atmosphere, the delicious food, Ole Norm's pass arounds and those big cinnamon rolls." He patted his stomach. "Eating don't get any better than that."

"Be sure to put Lambert's down as *the* place to eat when we're in this area," the prince said.

The limousine became their home over the next few weeks with them stopping only to eat, sleep, and perform.

Roseanna's reputation preceded her; in every city she performed to a standing-room-only crowd. Fans scrambled to get her autograph. Reporters vied for her attention. She felt a twinge of regret when the tour ended in late November and they headed home.

It was after midnight when they pulled into Nashville, but Roseanna couldn't sleep. She eagerly scanned the mail for letters from home. She read the ones from Brad first. Tears filled her eyes when she read how he had come to Nashville to take her home.

"Oh, baby, I'm sorry, I didn't know," she whispered, wiping the tears away.

In his other letters he spoke of his love for her, how much he missed her and how he hoped she would be home for Christmas.

Christmas. She had not thought about the holidays. Maybe she would go home.

"Prince, do we have any plans for Christmas?" she asked the next morning at breakfast.

"What did you have in mind, baby?"

"I thought I might go home for the holidays," she said.

"We have a lot of things to do but we'll try to work it out," he promised, knowing full well the promise would never be kept. He'd make sure of that.

Maurice smiled. "I'll drive you, Miss Roseanna," he said. "If that's okay with you, J.T."

"That's fine," he said, "but now Roseanna and I have a couple of things to go over before I leave for work."

"I'm ready," she said.

"We need to get your new album recorded right away," he told her. "It needs to be out by January One. I predict your 'Dreams' song will be number one on the charts by February."

"That soon?"

He nodded. "You'll need eight songs for the album. You can use the two you wrote while we were on tour. Do you have any others?"

She shook her head. "Not any that are suitable for the album."

"That means you'll have to come up with five more. That's a tall order, baby, but your fans are screaming for that song, and we don't want to disappoint them."

"I'll work day and night if I have to. I'll finish them on time."

"Thank you, darlin'. I hate to put this on you right now but time is of the essence. We also need a picture of you to send to the fans. I'll be back later with a photographer. Wear the black western suit and a bright scarf around your neck." He kissed her on the forehead and walked out the door.

The days passed quickly as Roseanna worked tirelessly, trying to finish the songs before Christmas.

"How's it going?" Maurice asked her one morning at breakfast.

"It's two weeks before Christmas, the songs aren't finished and I haven't even started my Christmas shopping," she sighed wearily.

"Grab your coat, darlin', we're going shopping," the prince said, taking her hand and pulling her to her feet.

"I can't—the songs."

"The songs can wait. You need a break, baby. We'll take my car and make a day of it. I want to show you the Christmas lights tonight. Don't fix dinner for us Maurice, we'll be home late."

The mall with its festive atmosphere cheered up Roseanna as soon as she walked through the doors. The bustle of Christmas shoppers added to her excitement.

"Where do we go first?" the prince asked.

"I need to buy presents for all my family and Brad," she answered, "but I'm not sure how much money I've got."

He laughed. "You've got all the money in the world if you need it, baby. If you see something you want, don't worry about the price, just buy it."

"I've got that much money?" she asked excitedly.

"Yeah, with your album selling like hot cakes and the money from the tour, you could buy the moon if

97

you wanted to, darlin'. We'll put it all on my credit card and settle up later."

She was like a kid in a toy shop. By mid-afternoon she had bought gifts for everyone back home.

"We'd better get these in the mail," the prince suggested, "in case a winter storm hits at Christmas and we get snowed in."

"Do you think that'll happen?" she asked, concerned.

"It's been known to," he said aloud. *But I'm not going to depend on it,* he thought to himself.

They found a place in the mall that wrapped and mailed packages and got the gifts in the mail.

"Are you hungry?" he asked.

"No, I'm too excited to eat," she said. "Would you help me find gifts for Mavis and Maurice and the guys in the band? That is if you're not hungry right now."

He shook his head. "We'll have an early dinner, and then I'll take you on a tour of the Christmas lights."

The first shadows of night were settling in when they finished shopping.

"Let's eat," the prince said as they walked to the car. "I know this great place where they serve the best steaks in town, if that's okay with you, baby."

"That sounds wonderful," she said.

"I've never had so much fun shopping," Roseanna remarked later as they finished dinner. "I'm glad we came."

"It has been a good day," he agreed, "but the best is yet to come." He motioned for the waiter.

"Wow!" Roseanna repeated over and over as they drove through the residential sections of Nashville. Whole neighborhoods were lit up brightly with the symbols of Christmas.

"I've never seen so many lights," she exclaimed joyfully. "It's beautiful!"

"You ain't seen nothing yet, darlin'," he said, driving up a winding road that led to the top of a mountain a few miles outside of Nashville. He parked the car and left the lights on so they could see where they were going. They walked to the edge of the mountain and looked down on the city.

"It's awesome," she gasped, gazing in wonder at the millions of lights twinkling below.

"That's the Opryland Hotel," the prince said, pointing to a big cluster of lights.

"It's beautiful, even from way up here," she sighed.

The wind howling through the trees whipped around them. Roseanna shivered.

"Take my coat, baby," the prince offered.

"No, you'll freeze without it," she muttered through chattering teeth.

"At least let me shield you from the wind," he said, pulling her close to his side and wrapping his topcoat around both of them.

They stood quietly for awhile looking at the lighted city below.

Roseanna broke the silence. "That view is breath-taking," she muttered in awe.

"It's nothing compared to the view I have right here," he said softly. He took her in his arms and kissed her; a kiss filled with all the passion of the first ones. This time Roseanna pulled away—but slowly.

"I'm sorry," he cried. "I don't have the right to kiss you like that. Forgive me, Roseanna."

She nodded breathlessly. As they walked to the car she was still shaking; this time it wasn't from the wind.

A couple of days before Christmas, Roseanna walked into the kitchen fretting. "I may as well forget about going home, Maurice, I'll never get all this finished in time."

"Surely there must be a way," he said.

She shook her head fighting back the tears. "We start taping the day after Christmas, and I've still got to finish one song and practice with the band."

"I'm sorry, child, I know you had your heart set on going home for Christmas. Have you let your family know?"

"I'll call them right now," she said, on the verge of tears.

Maurice put his arms around her. "I'm sorry that your Christmas is ruined, Miss Roseanna."

"Not to worry," the prince interrupted, walking in on the conversation. "Roseanna, since I had to break the promise I made you, I've arranged a special surprise."

"What is it?" she asked eagerly.

"If I told you then it wouldn't be a surprise. Just have an overnight bag packed and ready. We'll leave here late afternoon on Christmas Eve. Now run along and finish your song. The band's coming over early tomorrow to begin practice."

Dark clouds hung heavy on the horizon as they got into the limo Christmas Eve.

"Tell me where we're going, please," Roseanna pleaded.

"All in good time, baby."

"Tell me, Maurice," she begged.

"My lips are sealed, Miss Roseanna."

"Close your eyes, darlin' and don't look til I tell you," the prince said as they headed out of town.

"Can I keep them open until we're almost there?"

"Nope, I want this to be a total surprise," he told her, putting his hands over her eyes.

A few minutes later they turned off the highway, made a couple more turns and stopped.

"Okay, baby, you can look now?" the prince said, taking his hands away.

"The Opryland Hotel!" She jumped out of the limousine squealing with delight. She stood, spellbound, gazing at the thousands of tiny white lights twinkling in the darkness. Words could not begin to describe its beauty.

"Thank you, Prince," she cried, as they walked into the lobby. "This is a wonderful surprise."

"Merry Christmas, baby," he said, giving her a friendly kiss and pointing to the mistletoe above their heads.

When they reached the suite the prince had reserved, he took three brightly wrapped gifts from his luggage and handed them to her. "Go ahead and open these," he said, "they're for tonight."

She opened the large package first. A red sequined gown lay inside. "It's gorgeous," she whispered, holding it up to her. The second package held shoes to match the gown. An evening bag was in the last package.

Roseanna thanked the prince and hurried to her room to get dressed. She returned shortly looking radiant.

"Whoa, baby," he said, "you take my breath away."

She smiled, curtsying.

"Here's something else for you," he said, handing her a small package.

"Another gift?" You've done too much already," she said, opening the package. Her eyes grew wide with wonder as she stared at the necklace and earrings inside.

"Rubies to match your gown," he said fastening the necklace around her neck. The earrings dangled from her ears as he clipped them in place.

"Now off to the celebration." He took her arm and they walked into the lobby, barely making it in time for the six o'clock ceremony of the Yule log.

It was a sight to behold. A cast of characters dressed in colorful medieval costumes were led into the lobby by a trumpeter. The ceremony lasted only a few minutes but in that short time the holiday spirit filled the room as carols were sung and happy smiles exchanged.

"Now for the main event," the prince said as they walked into the Presidential Ballroom which was home to the Down Home Country Musical Celebration.

A banquet fit for a king awaited them. After dinner, the Opryland performers entertained the crowd as they sang, danced, and acted out the holiday story on a stage-set that turned inside out and backwards to create each new scene. An orchestra accompanied the performers. The rest of the evening was spent dancing to down-home music.

When Roseanna awoke the next morning, her thoughts turned home. Grandma would be in the kitchen in a tizzy, putting the final touches on Christmas dinner. Mama and the girls would be over later. Brad was planning to be there but when her plans changed, he went home to be with his family.

A tear slid down her face as she visualized that scene in her mind. She could hear those dear voices as joyous laughter filled the house. She could see those precious faces as they glowed with the happiness of Christmas. They would miss her, but they would celebrate with joy the glorious birth of the Christ Child.

She wiped the tears away when the prince knocked on her door.

"Time to get up, baby," he called. "I've ordered room service."

"I've never had brunch before," Roseanna said, sampling everything on the table. "This is wonderful—last night was wonderful." She reached over and touched his hand. "Thank you for making my Christmas such a happy one."

He squeezed her hand. "It pleases me to make you happy, Roseanna."

After brunch, they took a leisurely stroll through the conservatory, a tropical garden covering several acres. They wandered under waterfalls and over streams. The jungle-like foliage intrigued Roseanna and she would have tarried longer but the prince pointed to his watch.

"Maurice will pick us up soon," he said. "He'll come straight here from the mission."

"Do they serve Christmas dinner to the homeless every year?"

"Yeah, and Maurice always helps out, He's big on helping others."

"I know," she said. "He's really something."

Maurice fixed Christmas dinner with all the trimmings for their celebration that night. They exchanged gifts, and Maurice read the Christmas story from Luke. Roseanna played the guitar, and they sang carols rounding out the holiday in a joyous way.

Roseanna called home before going to bed, and talked to all of them. It didn't take the place of being there, but just hearing their voices warmed her heart and made Christmas a little brighter.

The next few days were busy ones with everyone working feverishly on Roseanna's album, trying to meet the deadline for its release.

"We did it, baby!" the prince exclaimed early New Year's Eve. "Your album is finished and all ready to go as soon as we get back."

"Back from where?" she asked.

"We're flying to New York City! We're ringing in the new year in Times Square, baby! Hurry, our plane leaves in an hour."

"I'm not packed."

"There's no time to pack. We'll buy everything we need when we get there."

"Wow," she muttered as they rushed out the door.

Magical things begin to happen as soon as Roseanna's feet touched the streets of New York City. Not even in her dreams had she imagined it would be like this.

"Oh, my," she gasped as she stood there gazing in wonder.

"We've got to get checked in, baby," the prince said, dragging her towards the hotel. She was so busy looking up at the tall buildings, she didn't seem to notice.

They shopped in the most famous stores in New York City, the ones Roseanna had read about in magazines.

"I can't wear this!" she cried, modeling a black gown with a close-fitting mini-skirt and a low-cut neckline.

"Relax, baby, it looks great on you and besides this goes with it," he said, handing her a floor-length white mink cape. "We wouldn't want you catching your death of cold."

They drove along Hudson Bay and stopped to view the Statue of Liberty. Roseanna stood in awe as she looked at the Grand Lady standing there in the harbor.

They dined in the finest restaurant, and danced to orchestra music afterwards.

Now, a few minutes before midnight, they were standing in Times Square, waiting for the countdown to begin.

Excitement, with the ferocity of a lightning bolt ready to strike, filled the air as the crowd watched the clock tick down the final seconds til midnight.

"10-9-8-7-6-5-4-3-2-1" they shouted.

"This is it, baby!" the prince yelled. On the stroke of midnight he pulled her into his arms and kissed her; a kiss that spoke of more than friendship.

Caught up in the fervor of the moment, Roseanna kissed him back.

Chapter 10

The winter storm hit in all its fury late New Year's Day. It snowed all night and by morning Nashville was blanketed in white. Men on snowplows were out early, feverishly working to clear the streets in time for the rush hour traffic.

"Let's make a snowman!" Roseanna exclaimed, running into the kitchen.

The prince laughed. "Can we at least eat breakfast first?" he teased.

"You sure are excited child," Maurice said, setting a bowl of hot cereal in front of her.

"We don't get snow very often back home, maybe once every twenty years," she explained.

"It's a good thing our plane landed before this storm hit or we'd be stranded somewhere between here and New York City."

"How was the Big Apple?" Maurice asked.

"It was magical," Roseanna said dreamily. "I want to go back someday."

"We're going back soon, baby, for a concert," the prince said. "It's all set up. This time we'll get to see more of the sights and take in some Broadway shows."

"Will the storm delay the release of the album?" Roseanna asked.

"No, darlin', my staff took care of that while we were in New York City. Folks are listening to you even as we speak. Now, go get dressed, and let's build that snowman."

. She nodded and hurried from the room.

"Maurice, I called Marty Rhyne over in Denver, North Carolina, and ordered two tour buses for Roseanna and the band to travel in. They're top of the line and each one will accommodate twelve people. They'll be ready for the East Coast tour. I've lined up a couple of semis to carry the equipment. You'll be driving Roseanna's bus. I wouldn't trust her safety to anyone else."

"Thank you, J.T. I'll take very good care of her," Maurice assured him. "Who all will be going on our bus?"

"Roseanna, you, and me, of course," he answered. "Also, my secretary and Michelle; Roseanna's personal assistant."

Roseanna came scurrying back into the kitchen. "You coming with us, Maurice?"

"No, child. These old bones of mine don't like the snow and ice. You two run along and have fun."

Roseanna's emerald green snowsuit contrasted sharply with the pure whiteness surrounding them as she and the prince frolicked in the snow. As a finishing touch to the snowman, they put a happy smile on his face.

"A fine piece of art if I ever saw one," the prince said, stepping back to admire their handiwork.

"He can't be a nobody snowman," Roseanna reflected. "He's got to have a name."

"What's the perfect name for a fine snowman like him?" the prince mused.

. "He's soft and pudgy," she answered. "Let's call him Puff."

"I dub thee Puff," the prince said ceremoniously.

Roseanna picked up a snowball and hurled it at the prince, hitting him on the shoulder. He returned the fire and the fight was on. Snowballs whizzed through the air, hit and miss, as the two of them laughed and dodged each onslaught until they fell, breathless, on the ground.

"I give," the prince gasped.

"Me too," she panted.

They lay there a few minutes taking in big gulps of the cold winter air, trying to catch their breath. The prince revived first and stood up. He took Roseanna's hand and pulled her to her feet.

"We'd better get inside," he said between breaths.

As they walked through the lobby, strains of "It's a Matter of Dreams" drifted softly from the radio.

"Great song," the manager said.

Roseanna smiled warmly and nodded her thanks. The burning in her throat kept her from speaking.

Maurice was watching them out the window. "Drink this," he said as they walked in, handing each of them a mug of steaming hot chocolate. Now get out of those wet clothes before you both catch your death of cold."

"This takes me back," the prince remarked nostalgically, as they sat on Roseanna's couch, sipping the hot chocolate. "When I was a kid, every time I came home with a skinned knee, hurt feelings, or anything like that, Maurice always made a big mug of chocolate foaming with marshmallows; a few sips, and I felt better."

"It still does the trick," she agreed. "My throat feels better already."

"That's a relief," he sighed.

"Playing in the snow was fun," she said. "My whole life here is fun, one exciting thing after another."

"How does your life here compare to your old life back home?"

"There's no comparison! I've seen places and done things here that we only heard of or read about there. I could never go back to that kind of life, not for a long time, anyway."

Roseanna had opened the door to a plan the prince had been mulling around in his mind. He pouched on the opportunity.

"Where does that leave your preacher?" he asked.

"Brad? He knows I'm coming back to marry him. He'll wait for me."

"How long will you keep him waiting, Roseanna; a year—two—ten—til he's an old man? Is that fair to him?"

"I'm waiting for him, too," she pointed out.

"Yeah, but you're living the good life here; your days and nights are filled with fun and excitement. What does he have?"

Roseanna remembered last summer when Brad went away to Camp Meeting: how empty her days were; how lonely and lost she felt without him; and he was only gone a few days. Tears misted her eyes as she thought of Brad there alone, with empty days and nights stretching into more empty days and nights.

"It's not fair to him!" she cried. "Prince, when do I have some free time? When can I go home and marry Brad?"

"When you're ready to exchange all this for a wedding band," he told her.

"Can't I have both?" she asked tearfully.

He put his arms around her. "I don't think so, baby, not with the preacher. Think about it Roseanna, you're gone for months at a time. A preacher needs a wife who can be there by his side helping him in his ministry. I'm sorry, darlin'; but I don't think it would work."

"But I love him," she sobbed.

"Then give all of this up, go home and marry him," the prince said. "The choice is yours, baby, but you need to make it soon. It's not fair to keep him in limbo and it's not fair to keep me wondering whether this fortune I'm spending to make you the biggest star on the planet is gonna be all for nothing. I need to know you're committed to this dream of yours; you can have it all, baby, but you have to be committed one hundred percent. And by the way, which came first, the preacher or the dreams?"

Roseanna knew the only choice she had and it broke her heart. "I love Brad, but I can't give up my life here," she cried. "I'd suffocate back there."

"Then you've got to break it off now, Roseanna, for his sake, for my sake, for everybody's sake."

"I know, but it's going to be the hardest thing I ever did. I've got to think of the right words to say."

"It's got to be final, baby, don't leave him dangling."

Later, she wrote through tear-dimmed eyes.
Dear Brad,

I'm writing this to set you free from the promises we made to each other. Please go on with your life without me, for I can never be a part of your world again. This is my world now, this is where I belong. I'm happy, Brad, and I want you to be happy too. Give this locket and your love to someone else, someone who is worthy of them. A part of me will always love you and regret leaving you, but my life is here now, so I must say good-bye to you forever. Please don't hate me.

Roseanna

She unclasped the locket and held it close to her heart. She kissed it and dropped it into the envelope along with the letter. "Good-bye, my love," she whimpered mournfully, as if a part of her had died.

The prince took the envelope from her. "I'll mail it, darlin'." Once outside the door he read the letter . He heard Roseanna weeping bitterly. "You won't be crying long, baby. After I hold you in my arms and make love to you, you'll forget that preacher ever existed." He braved the icy streets to mail the letter before she changed her mind.

"I want this sent by certified and overnight mail," he told the postmaster. "And from now on, no one is to pick up our mail but me. I need to scan it to make sure Roseanna doesn't get hold of any offensive fan mail. There's a lot of weirdo's out there."

"Don't worry, J.T. I'll handle it myself."

The next day, Brad was working outside when the mailman turned onto the dirt road leading up to the church. "Hey, Sam," he yelled, "am I getting special treatment today?"

"I couldn't leave this in the mailbox, preacher, you gotta sign for it."

"Certified, must be important," Brad remarked, signing the form. "It's from Roseanna." He said good-bye to Sam and hurried inside.

A letter from Roseanna always made his day brighter. He longed to see her face and hold her in his arms, but for now a letter had to do. He opened it eagerly. The locket fell out. He picked it up and held it to his heart.

"No, sweetheart," he cried knowingly. Hands trembling, he read the letter. Each word tore his heart right out of him. A pain like he'd never felt before engulfed his entire being. "No, I won't give you up! I'll

fight for you til the day I die!" With all the love in his
heart, he answered her letter.

My dearest Roseanna,

How can I go on with my life without you when
you *are* my life. I could never hate you , my darling,
because my love for you consumes my entire being and
leaves no room for anything else. Hold on to that part
of you that loves me, sweetheart, for someday it will
bring you back to me. When that day comes, I'll be
here waiting and we can fulfill the promises we made.
Until then, I hold you forever in my heart and in my
prayers.

I love you always,
Brad

"I've got to mail this today," he muttered,
"tomorrow may be too late." He grabbed his coat and
drove into town. Roseanna must know as soon as
possible how much he loved her and that he would wait
forever, if necessary.

The prince saw the letter from Brad when he
picked up the mail a few days later.

"Let's see if you let her go," he mumbled. He
drove to a near-by park, opened the envelope carefully
and read the letter. "Roseanna can never see this," he
snapped. "There's only one thing to do." He turned the
car around and drove across town stopping at a two-
story red brick house.

"Mel, I need your special talents," he told the
short, stout man who opened the door.

"Sure, J.T., what can I do for you?"

The prince handed him the letter, "I need you to
rewrite this using the words I give you."

Mel studied the letter carefully. Like an artist at
work, he copied, in Brad's handwriting, the words the
prince told him to write.

The prince looked it over. "Great job, Mel," he said, handing him five one hundred dollar bills.

"That takes care of you, preacher man," he snorted as he headed home.

"I believe you've been waiting for this," he said, handing Roseanna the letter.

"It's from Brad, he knew I didn't mean that letter. He's writing to tell me he'll wait for me," she squealed happily, tearing open the letter and reading.

Roseanna,

Thank you for the letter setting me free from the promises we made. I know now we were never meant for each other. In the months we've been apart, I've met someone else and now I'm free to offer the locket and my heart to her. I will fondly remember you and the time we shared together. Good-bye and have a happy life.

Brad

"No," she gasped. "I love you, baby, please don't stop loving me." But he had, the letter said so; its words, cold and unfeeling, tore her heart right out of her. *I'll remember you fondly.* That's all she was to him now—a fond memory.

"Prince, hold me," she cried. She needed strong arms holding her, shielding her from this hurt that totally consumed her.

"I'm sorry, baby," he said, pulling her close and speaking words of comfort to her.

She wept in his arms until there were no tears left inside her—only a big empty space where Brad's love used to be. He didn't love her anymore. She had to accept that and get on with her life. She had to forget him.

"Prince, do we have a tour scheduled soon," she asked, wiping the last tears from her face. "I'm going to put all my time and effort into my singing—it's all I have left now."

"We have some concerts in the area until the weather breaks, then we head for the East Coast on tour. You're singing at the Opry every Saturday night until we leave."

"Good," she said, "I want to keep busy."

The weeks turned into months. The icy cold of winter melted in the warm sunshine that heralded in spring. Newness of life cascaded over the earth as blades of grass sprang up and the trees brought forth their green leaves once again. Bulbs that lay dormant in the ground burst through in hues of brilliant splendor. Plants that died in the winter freeze bloomed again and filled the air with their sweet fragrance.

Roseanna kept busy. She looked ahead to her future, the past was too painful. She tried to put it behind her, but her heart kept reminding her of the love she had shared with Brad; the love she had thrown away.

The tours were long and strenuous. They took her along the East Coast to New York City, and then north to the Canadian border. Now, they were back home in Nashville for a few weeks before heading out on tour again.

"Come with me, baby," the prince said excitedly, pulling her to her feet. "I've got something to show you."

"Where are we going?" she asked as they got in his little red sports car and headed out of town.

"Patience, darlin'," he said as he turned onto a winding road that led to the top of a mountain a few miles outside of Nashville.

"Is this the same mountain?" she asked.

Smiling like the cat who ate the canary, he nodded.

"Here we are, baby," he said stopping in front of a massive Victorian mansion. He got out of the car.

"It's like Mrs. Pecot's house," she exclaimed.

"Come on, baby, we're going in," he said opening the car door.

"No, we can't, we don't know these people," she protested.

"It's okay, they know we're coming."

"What on earth are you doing?" she whispered nervously as he took a key from his pocket and opened the door.

"Do you like it, darlin?" he asked when they got inside.

"I love it! It's gorgeous, but we'd better get out of here. These people are not at home and we're trespassing,"

"They're not at home because they don't live here anymore. They're selling the house and it's yours if you want it, baby."

"Oh! Oh!" she exclaimed running from room to room taking in the beauty of the house. "Of course I want it! It's perfect, but it must cost a fortune."

"Yes, it does, but just say the word and we'll buy it."

"Prince, I want this to be my house," she said.

"I thought we'd all live here, you, Maurice and me."

"Of course we'll all live here, I didn't mean that," she assured him. "It's important to me that I buy this house with my own money. You understand, don't you?"

"I guess so, as long as you're not putting me out on the street," he teased.

"How soon can it be mine?" she asked, her eyes sparkling.

"As soon as you sign this," he said, putting the contract in her hands. "I was sure you'd want the house, so I took care of all the legal work."

"Wow," she said, signing the papers, "this house is mine."

"And all the property surrounding it. We own a big piece of this mountain, baby."

They walked through all fifty rooms. The prince would have his own wing, Maurice would have one too.

"It's time to go," the prince said. But instead of getting into the car, he took Roseanna's hand and led her to the spot where they had stood and looked at the Christmas lights.

"I want to talk to you, Roseanna," he said in a serious tone. "The last time we were here, I kissed you when I didn't have the right to. Now, I hope to have that right. I'm crazy about you, baby, and I want to be the man in your life, I know you're still hurting, but you've gotta go on with your life sometime. Why not now?"

Her heart cried no, but her mind took over. Brad had gone on with his life, it was time for her to move on too. She cared for the prince, and being with him was fun and exciting. If anyone could make her forget Brad, it was him.

"Of course you can be the man in my life," she said, moving into his arms and tilting her head to kiss him.

As they kissed, she thought of another kiss, long ago in the church yard, a kiss sweet and tender and full of love. A tear slid down her face.

Determined to erase that scene from her mind she kissed the prince again. This time his kiss was rough and demanding. It scared her. She pulled away.

116

"We'd better go now," she said. "Maurice will be worried."

Reluctantly, he let go of her.

"Start packing, Maurice," she exclaimed, running into the kitchen. She told him about the house on top of the mountain.

He beamed. "It's good to see you happy again, Miss Roseanna."

"That's not all the good news," the prince said grinning from ear to ear. "Roseanna and I are an item, we're going steady, I guess you'd say."

Maurice looked at her.

She nodded, smiling. "I've moped around too long. It's time I start living again."

Roseanna spent every free minute furnishing the mansion. She started with the rooms they would be living in, and finished them in time for them to move in before they left on tour.

Roseanna was on top of the world when she was on stage performing or when she was with the prince; but when night settled in around her, before sleep overtook her, her thoughts carried her back home. Pictures of Brad flashed before her eyes. She could feel his arms around her. She could taste the sweetness of his kiss, and even though she'd never admit it out loud, she knew she had thrown away the things that really mattered and she could never get them back again.

She jumped out of bed and begin writing.

He can never go back home, he's just a lonely cowboy,
He's been riding trails forever, he's been caught out in the rain.

"I know how you feel," she whispered tearfully, as feelings of loneliness engulfed her. She would finish the song later; right now the words were too painful. She fell across the bed and cried herself to sleep.

Chapter 11

"We're going to Vegas, baby," the prince shouted, bounding into the room. "I just got off the phone and it's all set."

"But we just got home," Roseanna complained. "I was hoping to get a chance to enjoy our house before leaving again."

"There will be time for that later. Vegas is the brass ring, baby, we've got to grab hold of it while we can."

"When do we leave?" she sighed wearily.

"The concert's in two weeks," he answered. "That will give you a few days at home. I called Mavis. She's coming right over to work on your new wardrobe."

"I have closets full of beautiful things, I don't need more," she said.

"Vegas is a special place, darlin', and I want you to have a special wardrobe, so don't argue."

"You're spoiling me," she said sweetly, putting her arms around his neck and kissing him, "but I love it."

Mavis arrived just then carrying several gowns. "I think these will be perfect," she said, following Roseanna into the dressing room off her bedroom.

Roseanna modeled gown after gown while Mavis pinned and marked them for alterations.

"J.T. tells me you two are dating," she remarked. "What happened to your preacher back home?"

"He's moved on with his life," Roseanna said and told her the whole story.

"I see," Mavis said thoughtfully. "Be careful, Roseanna, J.T. is older than you and he's been around, don't let him talk you into doing something you wouldn't normally do."

"He's not like that at all. He's a real gentleman. He'd never take advantage of me."

"How much do you know about men?" Mavis asked bluntly.

Roseanna laughed. "Mama had that talk with me when I was twelve. Don't worry Mavis, I made a promise to myself not to have sex until I'm married, and that promise is important to me. I'm not going to break it."

"Good for you," Mavis said. "By keeping that promise you'll save yourself a lot of grief," She hesitated a moment then went on: "I've never told anyone this, Roseanna, but I think you need to hear it. I was once like you, innocent and trusting, but I know how quickly that can change."

"What happened?"

"I met this man. He was everything I'd ever dreamed of, my Prince Charming. One look at him, and I was swept off my feet. Things got serious between us and he spent more time at my apartment than he did at his place. Everything was wonderful until I found out I was pregnant."

"You have a child?" Roseanna blurted out.

"No," Mavis said, quietly, tears filling her eyes. "When I told the man about the baby he became furious and told me to get rid of it."

"Get rid of the baby? I don't understand..."

"He told me to have an abortion."

120

"You didn't," Roseanna gasped, horror-stricken.

"Yes, I did," Mavis cried, "and I haven't had a moments peace since. When it was over, I felt dead and empty inside. Not a day goes by that I don't grieve for that child who will never know the simple pleasures of life. Not knowing whether I would have had a son or daughter makes the pain twice as bad. Sometimes I think of that little boy who will never throw a baseball, or climb a tree or come home with a frog in his pocket." Tears were trickling down her face, as she continued. "Other times I think of a little girl who will never have a tea-party; never pick wild flowers and bring them to me, or never dance in a ballet. I cheated my child out of those things, Roseanna. I killed my baby, a life that I helped create, a part of me, an innocent victim. I was its mother. I should have protected my baby, but instead I chose to take away its right to live, and I can never forgive myself for that."

Roseanna wept, holding Mavis in her arms. "It's that man's fault! He made you do it!" she cried angrily.

"I can't put all the blame on him, Roseanna. He didn't drag me down to that clinic. I blamed him at first and my love for him turned to hate. I don't hate him anymore but in the ten years since it happened I've never trusted another man."

"Not all men are like that," Roseanna said, brushing tears away. "My Brad is kind and gentle, he'd never..." she stopped, he wasn't her Brad anymore; he belonged to that world she'd left behind.

She clung to Mavis, weeping not only for Mavis's loss, but for hers as well. "Thank you for sharing this with me," she said. "I'm more determined than ever to keep the promise I made."

The prince knocked on the door. "May I come in?" he asked

They quickly wiped their tears.

'We're all finished here and I've got to be going," Mavis said. "J.T., I need to talk to you."

"Sure, baby, I'll walk you to your car," he said, taking her arm.

When they were outside, Mavis asked straight out, "J.T., what about Roseanna? What are your plans for her?"

"Well, before I'm through, she's gonna be Queen of country music," he said, a little puzzled by the question.

"That's not what I mean," Mavis snapped. "What are your plans for her in a personal way?"

"I'm crazy about that girl," he replied, "but why are we having this conversation?"

"Roseanna is sweet and innocent, I'd hate to see someone take advantage of her."

"I'm here to make sure that don't happen," he said tartly.

'Who's going to protect her from you, J.T.? I've seen you in action. Over the years I've watched you parade girl after girl through my shop, using them until you got tired of them, and then tossing them aside. I won't let you do that to Roseanna!" she stormed.

Anger flashed in his eyes. "Roseanna's not in the same ballpark as those other girls; she's in a league all by herself, and for you to suggest that I would use her..."

"I know you, remember? I've seen you operate and I'm warning you, J.T., don't you mess with that girl's head." Not waiting for him to answer she spun out of the driveway.

"Mavis sure is in a strange mood," he said, walking into the house. "What did you two talk about?"

"Just girl stuff," Roseanna said.

The prince took her in his arms and started to kiss her.

She pulled away. "Don't touch me!" she cried, storming out of the room.

"What's wrong with her?" he fretted. "She was fine before Mavis came over, now they're both in a foul mood." A frown crossed his face. "I won't let anyone, not even Mavis, come between Roseanna and me."

Roseanna came back into the room. "I'm sorry about before," she cried, running into his arms. "It had nothing to do with you. I was upset with men in general and I took it out on you. Please forgive me."

"What did Mavis say to upset you so, darlin'?"

"I can't tell you that," she said. "Please hold me; I need to feel your arms around me."

He held her close, stroking her hair and whispering words of comfort to her.

"You're such a kind, wonderful man," she muttered, looking into his eyes. "I'm lucky to have you in my life."

"I'm the lucky one, baby," he said, showering her with kisses.

"Opps, sorry," Maurice said, walking into the room. "I don't mean to disturb you, but dinner's on the table."

"We'll be right in, Maurice," the prince said. "Do you feel up to eating, baby?" he asked Roseanna.

She nodded.

As they walked into the dining room, hand in hand, Roseanna felt a twinge of guilt; she didn't love the prince the way he loved her. Love for Brad was still locked deep in her heart. A love that was lost forever, yet refused to let her go. Brad didn't love her anymore, she had to accept that and put him out of her heart so she could be free to love again.

She looked at the prince. He was the man in her life now. He deserved all of her love.

"I will love you the way you deserve to be loved," she silently vowed. "One day my heart will be yours alone, I promise." She squeezed his hand tenderly and pausing momentarily, she leaned over and kissed him.

Chapter 12

Roseanna's heart was not so restless now that she had resolved to put Brad in the past where he belonged and concentrate on falling in love with the prince.

Her heart was filled with anticipation as she got ready for the upcoming tour. They would go on to Hollywood from Vegas. The prince had lined up a concert there. She'd always dreamed of going to Hollywood one day and now she was actually going.

The song, "Lonely Cowboy", was tailor-made for Vegas, so she finished it and practiced with the band. Aside from the usual disagreements with Arlen, things went smoothly, and after a couple of sessions they were ready.

"How's the plans for the tour coming along?" Roseanna asked a couple of days before time to leave.

"Everything for the concerts is all set, and I've put Harriet in charge of the trip itself."

She laughed. "With your secretary in charge, heaven help the rest of us."

Harriet, a tall, powerful, aggressive woman would have been an Amazon in another time, another place. She had all the makings of a female warrior. She was a woman of action and clockwork precision.

She planned the trip to Vegas down to the smallest detail. Nothing was left to chance.

Maurice would lead the way, driving Roseanna's bus; the band would follow in the second bus, stopping only when Maurice stopped. They would make the trip in three days, traveling one-third of the distance each day. She had made advance reservations for the two nights they would be on the road. They would eat breakfast each morning before leaving the hotel, they would eat lunch on the buses (she had stocked the refrigerators amply), they would eat the evening meal at restaurants along the way. The only other stops they would make would be for fuel and to refresh themselves. There'd be no dawdling on this trip.

"Listen up, folks," she announced as they prepared to leave. "I have brochures from Vegas. Look them over. We'll have one free day before the concert and we want to take full advantage of it, so decide now what you want to do. That way, we won't waste any time when we get there. Any questions?"

They shook their heads. No one would dare challenge her plans.

"Is she always this organized?" Roseanna whispered to the prince.

"Right down to the last paper clip," he whispered back. "That's why my office runs so smoothly."

"Do you have anything to add, boss?" Harriet asked.

"Carry on, darlin', you're doing fine."

By the time they reached Vegas, their plans were set. Maurice would take the ladies to Hoover Dam and Red Rock Canyon. The men had planned a big day at the casinos.

The ladies were up bright and early the next morning, loaded down with cameras, bottles of water, hats, sunglasses and sunscreen lotion. Harriet clutched her trusty note pad in her hand.

"Have fun, baby," the prince said giving Roseanna a kiss.

"Sure," she grumbled. "With make-every-minute-count-Harriet calling the shots, how can we miss?"

He laughed. "At least you'll stay on schedule," he teased. He kissed her again and waved good-bye as they walked to the rental car and drove away.

The prince took a quick shower, got dressed, and was headed out the door when the phone rang.

Jay's voice was muddled and agitated. "Boss, I'm at the bus. You'd better get down here. We've got big-time trouble; it's Arlen."

"I'll be right there."

Jay was standing by the bus, pale as a ghost.

"What's he done this time?" the prince asked angrily. "I swear that man's gonna be the death of us all." He stepped into the bus then drew back in horror. "Is he...?"

"Yeah, he's dead," Jay said, his voice choking. "Looks like he OD'd on crack."

"How did this happen?"

Jay shook his head. "I don't know. Last night Arlen said he was too keyed up to sleep, that he was going out to look for some action. We thought he was going to the casinos to gamble, so we weren't concerned when he stayed out all night. This morning I came down to the bus and found him. What are we gonna do, boss?"

The prince thought for a moment. "We've got to leave everything just the way we found it," he said.

"But they'll know he's into drugs," Jay pointed out.

127

"They'll know anyway. If the needle marks on his arms don't give it away, the autopsy will. If we get rid of all this stuff, they'll come looking for the person who moved it, since Arlen certainly couldn't have."

"I see what you mean," Jay said.

"This is one big mess," the prince scowled, "but we can get through it if we all stick together. When the police questions you, just tell the truth plain and simple like you told me, and tell the other guys to do the same."

"Will do, boss,"

"There's none of this stuff lying around that will point the finger at us, is there?"

"No, everything is clean. We made sure of that before we got to Vegas."

"Good," the prince said, taking his phone from his pocket and dialing 911.

In a matter of minutes the hotel parking lot was swarming with police cars. Within a few seconds the area was roped off, and an officer was posted to keep curious onlookers away. Another officer was busy taking pictures of the body and the crime scene. A third went through the bus sprinkling powder everywhere a fingerprint might hide, hoping to find a set of prints foreign to the ones that would normally be there.

The man in charge walked over to the prince. "I'm Lieutenant Davis," he said flashing his badge. "Are you the one who called this in?"

"Yes, I'm J.T. Prince, Roseanna's manager. Arlen is—was the lead guitarist in her band."

"*The* Roseanna—Queen of country music?" the Lieutenant asked in astonishment.

"Yeah, her name's right there," the prince said, pointing to the side of the bus.

"I didn't notice. Where is she?" he asked, looking around hoping to get a glimpse of her.

"My chauffeur took the ladies to Hoover Dam and Red Rock Canyon for the day."

"I'll need to talk to all of them as soon as they return."

"Sir, Roseanna's going to be devastated by this. May I please be the one to tell her?"

"Sure, I don't see why not, but I will have to talk to her later."

Just then a heavy-set, clean shaven man arrived, carrying what looked like a doctors kit.

"The coroner?" the prince asked.

"Um-huh," the Lieutenant grunted. "Now what can you tell me about this?"

"Not much," the prince answered truthfully. "I didn't see him after we got to our suite last night. The first I heard of it was this morning when Jay called me. He found the body."

"Who's Jay?"

"He's the drummer in the band."

"I'll need to talk to him and the other members of the band. I'll also need to search their rooms."

"They'll cooperate in any way they can," the prince assured him.

"Can you tell me anything about the dead man that might help?"

"Aside from having an attitude problem he was a super guy. I never dreamed he was on drugs." He shook his head. "Such a waste; he had a great career ahead of him and a lovely wife and two great kids. Oh, no," he gasped, "his family—they don't know."

"You want us to take care of it?" the Lieutenant asked kindly.

"No, they should hear it from me," the prince said. "Maybe I can soften the blow a little."

The coroner walked up. "I'm finished here," he said. "From my preliminary examination I'd say he died from an overdose of cocaine. I'll know more after the autopsy."

The prince felt a sickening thud in his stomach as they rolled Arlen out in a black zippered bag. He turned his head.

"Are you finished with me?" he asked, his voice cracking. "I need to call his family before they hear it on the news. I've also got to find a replacement for him. In spite of how we feel the concert must go on."

"Yeah, we'd have a riot on our hands if you canceled it," the Lieutenant told him. "It's a sold out house already. My son is crazy about Roseanna. He'd give anything to go to that concert, but there's not a ticket to be found anywhere."

"I'll send tickets and backstage passes to you at your office. Let me know how many you need," the prince said, "that is, if it wouldn't be considered improper."

"I'll be a hero in my son's eyes if I get him to that concert, so I will take the tickets, but I'll pay for them; that way no one will have a problem with it."

"Okay, it's done," the prince said. "The backstage passes are free. Now if I can just find a good guitarist in time for the concert."

"I've heard of a local man who is supposed to be the best around. I haven't heard him myself, but some of the guys down at the precinct swear by his music. He's a little down on his luck and lives at a nearby mission. He works there for room and board. He picks up jobs playing at local nightclubs when he can. I'll get his address for you."

"Thank you," the prince said, shaking hands with the Lieutenant.

"We had fun today," Roseanna exclaimed bounding through the door late that afternoon.

"Hoover Dam was so impressive. We rode an elevator way down underground where the workings of the dam are located. A guide showed us through and explained it all to us. Then we drove through Red Rock Canyon and stopped at this ranch, it's sorta like a museum.." she stopped. "Prince, you're not listening."

"Come, sit down, baby," he said leading her over to the couch. He had a strange look in his eyes.

The color drained from her face. "Something's wrong—is it Mama..."

He stopped her. "No, darlin', everything's fine there. It's Arlen—he's dead."

"No," she gasped. "How? When?"

His voice choked as he told her the story.

"No, not drugs," she cried. "I didn't know he..."

"None of us knew he was a user, baby," the prince said. He held her in his arms. "I'm so sorry this happened."

"I guess the concert's off," she said tearfully.

"No, baby, we've got to go on with the show no matter how much we're hurting. The fans are depending on us."

"But how can we, without Arlen?"

"I've found a man to take his place. His name is Lee. He's a fan of yours. He has your albums so he already knows how to play all of your songs except the new one. I left a tape for him so he can practice. He'll get together with the band tomorrow."

"But how can I get up on that stage and sing, especially that new song, knowing Arlen is dead?"

"You're a trooper, baby, and that's what troopers do; they keep on going no matter what, cause the show must go on."

The prince stepped out on the stage the following night. "Welcome folks," he said. "I'm J.T. Prince,

Roseanna's manager. I'm sure you've heard about our tragedy. I apologize for it. We're all devastated by it but we feel we must go on with the show—Arlen would have wanted that." He motioned for Roseanna.

The auditorium exploded with applause as she walked out on the stage.

"Thank you," she said smiling sweetly. She nodded to her band and started singing. Her voice broke a few times during the first song but the entertainer in her soon took over and she sang song after song, delighting the audience in her usual manner.

She took a bow and ran off stage as a group of young dancers came on to perform while she prepared for the show's finale.

"Quick, Michelle, help me," she said, as she slipped out of the icy blue gown and into a red silk blouse. She pulled on a black leather mini-skirt and matching vest. She tied a bright colored scarf around her neck and changed her high-heeled shoes for black leather boots.

"How do I look?" she asked as Michelle brushed her cheekbones with a hint of blush and smoothed out her hair.

"You're going to knock them dead in that outfit," Michelle answered.

"I don't know how I'm going to get through the new song, it reminds me of Arlen," she said, pouring liquor, that the prince had brought, into a small glass.

"You're not going to drink that!" Michelle exclaimed horrified.

"A sip or two won't hurt anything and I need it to get through this song.," Roseanna said, drinking it down. She handed the empty glass to Michelle and ran back on stage as the dancers finished their act.

The audience was in a frenzy. Whistles echoed around the room. Men stood and cheered.

Roseanna blushed but she felt a bit pleased at all the attention she was getting.

"Thank you," she yelled, as the crowd quieted down. "I wrote this song especially for tonight, "It's called "Lonely Cowboy" and I hope you like it."

Thoughts of Arlen and the life she'd left behind flooded her mind as she sang the song. Tears flowed down her face.

Now he can never go back home, he's just a lonely cowboy,
He's been riding trails forever, he's been caught out in the rain;
And the snow covers quickly the footprints of a drifter,
And the wind it blows a chill so cold that it almost kills the pain;
And the tumbleweeds roll by him like ole memories of somethin',
That got lost along the rivers that flow across the plains of time;
And the voices in the midnight that still haunt the lonely campfire,
Only serve as reminders of his many sad good-byes.
And he tries to find some comfort in the night,
And he remembers back when once he thought he saw the light;
Oh, if he'd only done things different years ago,
He might have something now that he could show;
For a life that's just been wasted on the way,
And if there was only something he could say;
Besides I'm sorry, then I reckon it would be,
Say you've got to serve the Savior,
You need to serve the Savior;
I wish I had served the Savior,
But instead I only served me.

Now that ole forty-five is a rusty worn out shooter,
And those saddle bags that once were full now just
hang empty by his side;
And the spurs that used to jingle have gone quiet
in the desert,
That has now become his prison like the one deep
down inside;
And the dreams of the good life that led down
endless highways,
Have dwindled into nothing and they've left
nothing to his name;
And all the treasures he went after have long since
gone and wasted,
And the life that he was given he will never live
again.
And he tries to find some comfort in the night,
And he remembers back when once he thought he
saw the light;
Oh, if only he'd done things different years ago,
He might have something now that he could show;
For a life that's just been wasted on the way,
And if there was only something he could say;
Besides I'm sorry, then I reckon it would be,
Say, you've got to serve the Savior, little boy;
You need to serve the Savior, son,
I wished I had served the Savior;
But instead I only served me.
You've got to serve the Savior, little girl,
You need to serve the Savior, honey;
I wished I had served the Savior when I had a
chance.
But like a fool I only served me. I only served me

She took a bow as she finished the song.

134

The audience stood, tears in their eyes cheering loudly. The applause lasted for several minutes and when it finally died down, a young man sitting on the first row yelled: "I'd gladly trade places with that lonely cowboy if you'd be my little cowgirl. I'd trade my soul for a kiss from you.

The liquor was taking effect and Roseanna was in a playful mood. "We wouldn't want you doing that," she said, walking down off the stage.

The security guards rushed over to her.

"It's okay, he's harmless," she said smiling at the guards. She walked over and gave the young man a friendly kiss.

He grabbed her and kissed her long and hard. The guards pulled him away from her.

"With a kiss like that, he won't be lonely for long," Roseanna said, laughing and walking back on the stage. She took a final bow, and with the applause of the audience ringing in her ears, she ran off the stage and back to the dressing room.

The prince was there waiting. His face was flushed with anger. He grabbed her and shook her violently. "You little tramp!" he screamed.

"But you told me to wear this," she cried, trying to break free from his grasp.

"I didn't tell you to parade around like a two-bit whore," he fumed, tightening his grip on her.

"Stop, you're hurting me!"

"I saw you crying, singing about that religious stuff—you were thinking about that preacher," he stormed. "I ought to..." he raised his fist to hit her.

The door flew open and the new man in the band bolted in. Rage showed on his face. His fist hit the prince's chin and sent him sprawling across the floor.

"You touch my daughter again and I'll kill you!"

Roseanna whirled around and looked at the man standing there.

"Daddy?" It was more of a whimper than a question.

He grabbed her and pulled her into his arms, embracing her as tears ran down his face and dropped onto her shoulders. "My precious baby," he said. "My sweet Roseanna."

"Daddy," she whispered again, holding on to him tightly, feeling safe in his arms like she did when she was a little girl. Suddenly she pushed him away. The hatred she'd felt for him all these years came flooding over her.

"You left us!" she screamed. "You broke Mama's heart and mine too. I loved you so much; we all did, but you threw us away like we were nothing more than garbage!"

"Roseanna, please give me another chance," he begged.

"No! Get away from me, I hate you!" She pushed past Maurice, who was now standing in the doorway, and ran blindly down the hall.

The prince ran after her.

"Don't you hurt her again or you'll answer to me!' Ellis LeBlanc shouted angrily.

Maurice didn't know what was going on but he was sure going to find out. "Come on, Lee, I'll drive you home," he said.

The prince caught up with Roseanna and though she fought him like a tiger, he got her into the limousine he had rented for tonight. He frowned. Things were not going the way they were supposed to. He had planned a big night with Roseanna in the city where the lights never go out. They would dine at one of Las Vegas finest restaurants then go from one nightclub to another catching the shows and dancing til dawn. He might even tell her he loved her. But instead, here they were, on their way back to the hotel where he hoped to undo the damage he'd done tonight. Could she ever forgive him?

When they were inside the suite he put his arms around her to comfort her.

She cringed. "Don't touch me," she said backing away from him.

He had never heard such a coldness in her voice. It hurt him to know he had put it there.

"Baby, I'm sorry I hurt you tonight. You've got to know I didn't mean those hateful things I said to you. I flew into a jealous rage when those men looked at you that way. You could never be those things I called you. You're the closest thing to an angel there is on this earth, and I am the most loathsome creature ever. I wouldn't blame you if you hate me, Roseanna. I hate myself for what I did to you tonight. I don't deserve your forgiveness, but I'm begging for it." He reached and took her hands. "Please forgive me and don't hate me. You're the best thing in my life, baby, please let me make things right again. Don't shut me out, Roseanna, talk to me."

"I'm going to take a shower and we'll talk when I get back," she said with no emotion at all.

In a short time, she came back into the room wearing a yellow tee shirt and jeans. She sat down on the couch beside him. "I don't know if I can forget the things you said to me tonight or if I can forgive you, but because of all you've done for me I'm going to try, that's all I can promise."

"Thank you, baby, that's more then I deserve and I promise I'll spend the rest of my life making it up to you."

Her neck was tied up in knots. She rubbed it trying to get rid of the tension.

137

"Here, darlin', let me do that," he said, rubbing her neck and shoulders. He gasped in horror when he saw the marks on her arm—his hand prints—where he had grabbed her earlier. They were turning an ugly black.

"Roseanna, your arms!" he cried. "I didn't mean to hurt you, baby. If only I could take it back." He pulled her into his arms tenderly, and for the first time in years, he wept.

As Roseanna sat there in his arms, she remembered the good times they'd shared, the things he'd done to make her happy and she wept along with him.

The tears, like a cleansing rain, washed away some of her hurt and anger, leaving her so emotionally drained and exhausted that she fell asleep in his arms.

The prince eased her around, laying her down on the couch. He put a pillow under her head and a blanket over her.

"Baby, you're in no shape to be alone," he whispered, sitting down on the floor beside her. "I'm gonna stay here with you all night." He gently kissed the bruises on her arms, feeling a deep-down guilt, one that would last long after the bruises were gone. He cradled her in his arms and laid his head on the pillow beside her. He would watch over her tonight like a mother watches over a sick child. He had hurt her, physically and emotionally, and he didn't know if the scars would ever heal. He could only hope that in time they would.

Maurice came in a little while later. They were both asleep, the prince sitting on the floor holding Roseanna's hand. He started to wake him but decided against it. He turned out the light. "We've got some talking to do," he muttered quietly, "but it can wait til tomorrow."

Chapter 13

The morning light filtered into the room. Roseanna stirred. Her mind was foggy. She didn't remember going to bed last night. She turned her head and looked right into the face of the prince.

"What's going on?" she pondered out loud.

She raised up on her elbow and looked around. She was on the couch, the prince was sitting on the floor, asleep, with his hand resting gently on her arm.

As she looked at him her thoughts turned to their relationship. Was it over? Did she want it to be? She looked at the bruises on her arms; if he loved her so much how could he do that to her—Brad would never hurt her like that. She forced her thoughts back to the prince. It wasn't fair to compare him to Brad—no one could ever measure up to Bradley Lefourche.

The prince had to be judged on his own merits. Was it fair to judge him solely on his actions last night? Should that one incident blot out all the good in him. She recalled the good times they'd had, all the things he'd done for her. Did she want to give that up? What would her life be without him? She knew the answer. Her world would be drab and empty without the prince in it.

She shook him gently.

He opened his eyes and looked around. He tried to stand. "Ouch," he groaned, "my legs."

"I don't wonder," she said. "How long have you sat there?"

"All night," he moaned. "You went to sleep out here last night, and you were in no shape to be alone, so I stayed with you."

"We've got to talk about last night," she said.

"Darlin', I'm sorry I hurt you. I'd give everything I own if I could take it back, but I can't. I can only beg you to forgive me."

"I want to, but can I ever trust you again, or will I cringe every time you touch me?"

"Please don't be afraid of me," he pleaded. "I'd die before I'd hurt you again. I'll do anything to prove myself to you, Roseanna, just name it."

"All I want is for you to be that kind, loving man you were before last night, the man I was proud to have in my life."

"Oh, baby," he said, taking hold of her hands, "I promise that from this moment forward, I will be that man you want me to be."

"I'm going to hold you to that promise," she said. "I'll forgive you for last night and we'll put it behind us."

"Thank you, darlin'," he said.

Maurice walked into the room. "J.T., we've got to talk about last night."

Roseanna ran over and gave him a big hug. "We've talked already. Everything's okay."

He saw the bruises on her arm. His jaw twitched. Anger flashed in his eyes. "You did this to her!" he stormed.

Roseanna didn't give the prince a chance to answer. "It looks a lot worse than it really is, Maurice. Honest."

140

The phone rang. The prince answered it.

"I've forgiven him, Maurice, won't you please forgive him too?"

"I'll forgive him," he replied, "but I'll keep my eye on him. I won't let him hurt you again."

"Thanks for caring." She kissed him on the cheek.

"Miss Roseanna, there's someone else who needs your forgiveness. Can you find it in your heart to forgive your father?"

"No!" she cried. "I'll never forgive him! He left us with not so much as a dime to our name, with nothing more than a roof over our heads. He didn't even say good-bye."

"I feel certain no one regrets that more than him. When I drove him home last night he poured his heart out to me. I think he loves all of you very much."

"If he loved us why did he leave us?"

"You need to ask him that," Maurice said gently.

"I don't want to hear anything he has to say," she snapped.

"I think you must hear him out, child, for your own peace of mind. What he did was inexcusable but everyone deserves a second chance. Just say the word and I'll give him a call."

She nodded, reluctantly.

"That was Lieutenant Davis on the phone," the prince said. "They've completed the autopsy on Arlen's body. It wasn't an overdose exactly, he got hold of some almost pure cocaine and that's what killed him. They're certain it was self-injected, so we're all free to go. They'll keep the investigation open, hoping to find the person who sold him the cocaine."

"What happens now—to Arlen?" Roseanna's voice faltered.

"I've got to go sign the papers for the release of his body. I'll get all the details then." He kissed her and hurried out the door.

Maurice called the mission and talked to Roseanna's father. "I'm going over and pick him up. You won't regret this," he told her.

Roseanna changed her tee shirt for a long sleeved blouse. She didn't want her father seeing the bruises on her arms. She paced nervously until she heard a knock at the door. Mixed emotions raged inside her when she saw her father standing there alone.

"Maurice had to run some errands," he explained. "May I come in?"

She stepped back and motioned him inside. Her heart pounded furiously. What would she say to this man, her father, whom she'd hated all these years.

It was easy to see that he felt awkward too.

As she stood there facing him all the hurt and anger bottled up inside her came pouring out.

"Why did you leave me, Daddy?" she cried. "I was your little girl. We were special to each other. When you left, I ran to our special place and waited for you. I was sure you would come, but you didn't. I stood for hours looking down the road, expecting to see you come walking home to us. I told everyone you'd be back. I couldn't believe you would leave me."

"Roseanna, the hardest thing I ever did was to walk away from my family. You were the most precious things on earth to me."

"Then why, Daddy?"

"I honestly thought I was doing the best thing for all of you," he said with sadness in his voice. "You deserved so much more than I could offer you."

"But we loved you, Daddy. You were all we needed."

"No, baby, I was a loser. I never held a steady job; I didn't provide for my family; you deserved better than that. I can offer no excuse for what I did, and if I could go back and do it over..." his voice trembled, "leaving all of you was the biggest mistake of my life."

"Why didn't you come back to us, Daddy?"

"By the time I realized what I'd done it was too late. Without your mother's good influence in my life I hit bottom. I started drinking heavily and bummed around from bar to bar. I was in no shape to come back home to my family.

"But I still don't understand why you left Daddy—if you loved us so much."

"I don't understand it all either, baby, but I guess it was partly due to these feelings I had churning around inside me. As you know I was born on the bayou but I was raised in the city. I met your mother on a visit back home and fell madly in love with her. I moved to the bayou to be with her, but I never adjusted to the simple life there. I had this wander-lust spirit in me that made me want to see the world; it was a yearning that wouldn't let go of me; it kept pulling and tugging at me. I fought against it for years, but in the end it won out and I walked away from the ones I loved most in the world. I'm sure you don't understand this, Roseanna," he said, tears flowing down his face.

Roseanna's heart pricked within her. She understood it more than he knew. Grandma was right—she was her father's daughter.

He continued on. "I realized I could never be the man your mother deserved. I walked away so she would be free to find another love, someone who was worthy of her."

Roseanna's head whirled as she remembered the words she had written to Brad: *Give this locket and your love to someone else, someone who is worthy of them.* "Oh," she reflected, "did my words hurt him as badly as Daddy's leaving hurt Mama? No, he was glad I set him free." He'd moved on with his life. Mama never had—she still loved Daddy.

The walls of resentment and hatred that Roseanna had built up through the years came tumbling down. She ran into her father's arms and wept as the love for him that she had felt all those years ago came flooding back.

When her tears dried, Roseanna told Daddy about the family, about how desperately she'd wanted to get away from the bayou. She told him about Brad, tears misting her eyes, as she spoke of the love they'd shared. She told him abut the prince and Maurice and of her life as a country music star.

"You've made it big," he said, pride showing in his voice.

"I owe that all to you, Daddy, you taught me everything I know."

"Roseanna, are you sure this is the life for you?" he asked, a shadow passing across his face. "I don't like that Prince fellow, I don't trust him. Why don't you go back home and patch things up with your preacher?"

"It's too late for that," she said sadly. "Besides, Daddy, you don't really know Prince, he's not at all like what you saw last night. He's a kind, wonderful man who gives me everything a girl could want."

"I saw what he was giving you last night and if he ever lays a hand on you again, I will kill him."

The door opened and the prince walked in. He stared a moment at Roseanna's father, then walked over to him, and in a voice smooth as silk, he apologized.

"Sir, I'm sorry about last night. I hurt your daughter. I can offer no excuse for it. I can only promise that it will never happen again. I love Roseanna with all my heart, she's the most precious thing in my life, I cherish her." He paused a moment then said, "I'm thankful you burst into that room when you did, I even appreciate that punch you gave me. If you hadn't stopped me—if I had hit her," his voice broke. "Please forgive me, sir," he said, extending his hand.

Ellis LeBlanc refused to shake hands. "Roseanna says you're a nice guy, but I'm going to reserve my judgment of you 'til later," he said bluntly. "If I ever hear of you hurting her again, heaven help you."

"That's fair enough," the prince said, "but putting your feelings for me aside, how would you like a permanent job with the band?"

"Please say yes, Daddy," Roseanna urged.

"I'd love to darling, but I can't. I'm an alcoholic. The folks at the mission are helping me get my life back on tract. I haven't had a drink in weeks, but if I leave now, I'd be drinking again in no time."

"Okay," the prince said, "but the offer stands anytime you're ready."

"Daddy, why don't you at least go to Hollywood with us?"

"I could do that," he said.

"That will work out great," the prince said. "Baby, I've chartered a plane to fly Arlen's body back to Nashville. Harriet and I will go along to help with the arrangements and to be there for his family. We also need to do some PR work to make sure this doesn't affect you. I can breathe easier knowing your father will be with you."

"We'll leave sometime tomorrow, Daddy, I'll call you later with the details."

145

"That's fine, but now I've got to be going, " her father said, "it's almost lunch time." He gave Roseanna a big hug. "If you'll call me a cab..."

"Nonsense," Maurice said, walking in the door. I'll drive you."

"I don't know about doing a concert without you, Prince," Roseanna fretted after the two men left. "You always take care of everything. I only sing. I could never do all that other stuff."

"Folks come out to hear you sing, baby, they could care less about the other stuff."

"What if something comes up that I can't handle?"

"I can't imagine what it would be," he said. "The boys in the band will set up the equipment, an emcee will introduce you, and all that's left is for you to do what you do best—sing. What could possibly go wrong?"

"I feel better but I'm going to miss you." She snuggled close to him.

"I'll miss you too, baby," he said, kissing her as only the prince could.

"Wow!" she said, "that was some kiss. If we ever break up, I think that's what I'll miss most of all."

"We're not going to break up, baby. I'll never let you go," he vowed. "Now, if you'll excuse me, I've gotta make a phone call."

"Getting rid of me already?" she teased. "I'll start packing for the trip," she said, kissing him as she left the room.

When Roseanna was safely out of earshot, the prince dialed the phone.

"Law offices of Smith and Crandall. Good morning," a pleasant voice at the other end of the line answered.

"William Crandall, please. J.T. Prince calling."

"Just a moment, Mr Prince."

The prince tapped nervously on the phone while he waited.

"J.T., how's it going," the lawyer asked.

"I've seen better days," he told him. "I've got some urgent business I need you to take of."

"I heard about Arlen's death, does it have anything to do with that?"

"Not exactly, but it did get me to thinking. One little slip up and I could lose everything I own."

'We've been really careful, J.T., there's not going to be a slip up."

"You don't know how close we came here." He paused. "Here's what I want you to do. Put every I own in Roseanna's name."

"Man, that's crazy," the lawyer blurted out. "Do you realize what a chance you're taking? You could lose everything."

"I could lose it if I don't. My bank accounts, my stocks, my property, everything I own—one little mistake could wipe it all out. Draw up the papers, today, putting everything in her name and I'll sign them when I get home."

"I strongly advise against this.."

"It's my money," the prince snapped. "Just do it and keep it quiet. This is between you and me."

"J.T., as your lawyer and friend, I'm warning you, your playing with fire here..."

"Take care of it!" the prince stormed, slamming down the phone as Roseanna walked back into the room.

"What's that all about?" she asked.

"Nothing for you to worry your pretty little head about, baby. Just business."

The phone rang. It was Maurice. "I wanted to let you know that I'm going to stay at the mission and

147

help serve the evening meal, then I'm staying for church tonight. I'm the guest speaker. Don't wait up, I'll be late."

"Okay, Maurice, thanks for calling. Knock-em-dead at the service tonight."

"Maurice going to church tonight?"

"Yeah, at the mission. He's the guest speaker."

"I'd like to hear him. Maybe we can go," she said.

"If you were there, darlin' he'd lose his audience, they'd all be looking at you." He took her in his arms. "I guess it's just you and me tonight, baby. What would you like to do?"

"I'm not in the mood to get all dressed up," she said. "Why don't we order room service?"

"Sounds good to me." He picked up the phone and ordered their favorite foods from the menu.

They enjoyed a quiet, leisurely meal which was a luxury in itself amid the turmoil of the last few days.

"What would you like to do now?" the prince asked as the waiter removed the dishes from the room.

"I'm going to take a long hot bath and get into my pj's," she said.

"You're not going to bed this early," he said with surprise.

She laughed. "No, I'm going to get comfortable and sit here and listen to music for a while and just relax."

"That sounds great," he said. "I think I'll join you."

She came back about a half an hour later looking refreshed and fetching in white silk pajamas and matching robe.

"Come sit beside me," the prince said, patting the couch. He cradled her in his arms as they sat listening to soft music on the radio.

148

She twisted her neck from side to side. "That bath didn't get rid of all the kinks," she muttered.

"Turn around, baby, and I'll get rid of them."

"Hmmm, that feels good," she sighed, relaxing to the touch of his hands as he massaged her neck and shoulders.

"This will feel even better," he said, kissing her passionately.

Roseanna, basking in the thrill of his embrace, kissed him back.

"I want you, baby," he whispered. "I need you." His kisses became fiery, demanding.

"No." She pulled away from him. Roseanna was innocent and naïve but she knew he was wanting more than she was willing to give. "No," she whispered again, a look of pain in her eyes.

"Why, baby?" he asked, bewildered. "I thought you wanted this too."

Tears filled her eyes. "Try to understand, no matter how I feel, I can't do this. I shouldn't have let things go this far. I should have realized how it would affect you. I was thoughtless, I didn't consider your feelings and I'm sorry."

"I don't understand, baby. What's wrong?"

"I should have *told* you this up front; I'm not going to have sex until I'm married. I made that promise to myself. It's important to me and I'm not going to break it. It wasn't fair of me to let you think otherwise. Please forgive me."

"It's okay, darlin'," he said convincingly.

The prince couldn't risk pushing her further than she wanted to go. Last night was still too fresh in her memory. He had to bide his time. If he forced the issue now he could lose her forever.

"She wanted me tonight," he reflected silently, "but that promise stood in the way. Someday soon, I'll make her forget she ever made that promise, and then she will be mine."

Chapter 14

"Hurry, Roseanna, we're almost there," Michelle urged.

"What time is it?" Roseanna asked as she finished dressing.

"Two minutes later than last time," Michelle said. "Don't worry, we'll make it."

"If that restaurant where we ate lunch hadn't had that cute little gift shop, we wouldn't be in this mess," Roseanna grumbled. "I'd be dressing in a comfortable hotel room instead of on this bus."

"We would have made it okay if we hadn't got stuck in that five o'clock traffic. I doubt if Maurice will ever speak to us again."

"He was upset," Roseanna agreed. "I never thought I'd say this but we sure could use Harriet along about now."

"Bite your tongue," Michele snorted. "You didn't have to live with her day and night."

Roseanna laughed. "Bad, huh?"

Michelle nodded. "We went to bed by the clock, we got up by the clock. We did everything by the clock. She had it all written down in her little black notebook."

"Miss Roseanna," Maurice yelled, "we're pulling into the parking lot. I got you here with five minutes to spare."

He drove to the stage entrance and let the girls out.

"I'll check us in at the hotel and be back as soon as I can," he promised.

Roseanna ran into the concert hall just as the emcee walked out on the stage. She waved to let him know she was there. Relief showed in his face. "Ladies and Gentlemen, let's welcome Roseanna!"

Roseanna scampered out on the stage, smiling and waving to the audience. She burst into strains of "It's a Matter of Dreams", singing with all the gusto inside her. When she finished there was hardly a dry eye in the auditorium. The applause almost brought the house down. That song had been number one on the charts for months and it was a favorite everywhere she went.

"Thank you. Thank you," she said when the applause died down. "It's a pleasure to be here tonight. I've always wanted to come to Hollywood, and now I'm here. I'm going to sing some more of my songs for you. I hope you like them."

She thrilled the audience for over two hours, singing song after song. When she finished the last song of the night, the crowd stood and cheered. Roseanna came back on stage for a couple of encores, then she took her final bow. She hurried to the dressing room, the roar of applause ringing in her ears.

"You knocked-em-dead!" Michelle exclaimed joyously, hugging her.

"It did go well, didn't it?" Roseanna's voice was bubbly. "I didn't think I could do it on my own, but I did."

A knock sounded at the door.

"Maybe it's Maurice," Michelle said opening the door.

A tall gray-haired man stood there. He was good looking in a fatherly sort of way.

"May I help you?" Michelle asked politely.

"Yes," he answered, "I'd like to talk to Roseanna."

"Come in." Roseanna said, motioning him inside.

"I'm Parker Anderson", he said, "and I'll come right to the point. I'm a movie producer and I'd like to star you in the movie I'm getting ready to shoot."

"Me?" Roseanna gasped "Why me? I've never acted before."

"I believe you can do this one. It's called Bayou Girl, so I think you'd be a natural. Besides, I know how to take care of the acting part."

"I don't know," she said hesitantly. "My manager takes care of all the business and he's back in Nashville. I'll talk to him as soon as I get home, and we'll get back to you."

"I'd sure like to star you in this, but time is one luxury we can't afford," the producer said. "We've got to cast this right away. We start shooting in January, so I'll need to know in a few days, a week at the most."

"Leave the script with me and I'll read it over," Roseanna said. "I'll let you know within the week."

"I just happened to bring one with me, hoping you would agree to read it," he said smiling. He handed her his card. "I'll be waiting to hear from you."

Roseanna sat stunned for a moment, trying to take it all in. She sighed and shook her head. "Can you believe it? Me, a movie star?"

"And just think, I knew you back when…" Michelle mused dreamily.

"Oh, you," Roseanna laughed. "Let's get out of here and find Maurice." She picked up the script, they found an exit, and walked through the door.

They came face to face with a mob of young fans waiting there, hoping to get a glimpse of Roseanna. They rushed upon her, screaming and yelling. Some tried to touch her; one young man tried to cut off a lock of her hair.

Roseanna panicked. She wished the prince were here; he'd know what to do. But he wasn't here, she was on her own.

"Calm down," she murmured to herself. "These are your fans. Handle the situation." A young girl standing next to her held a guitar hoping to get Roseanna to autograph it. "Let me borrow this a second," Roseanna said. The girl handed it to her with a smile. Roseanna strummed it and started singing. The crowd quieted down to listen. She finished the song, autographed the guitar and handed it back to the girl.

"Now," she said to her fans, "I'll be happy to sign autographs for each of you, but you must line up and calmly tell me your names, one at a time. And I'd like to say to that young man who tried to cut my hair, please don't do that again. I like my hair just the way it is, but if you're ever in Nashville when I'm getting it trimmed, I'll gladly give you a lock of it for free."

The fans laughed and cheered, and a red-faced young man waved his hand. They lined up, and Roseanna spent the next half-hour signing autographs and talking to them.

"I've been looking everywhere for you two," Maurice scolded, walking up to them. "I was worried sick."

"We're sorry, Maurice," Roseanna said, waving good-bye to her fans and taking his arm. "We came out the wrong exit and there they were."

"It was a bad situation at first, but Roseanna handled it beautifully," Michelle told him.

"We'll talk about that later," Maurice said, "but now let's go to the hotel and get something to eat."

"I am famished," Roseanna said, "we haven't eaten since lunch."

"Over ten hours ago," Michelle said, looking at her watch.

"Your father's waiting at the stage entrance," Maurice said. "The band's pulling out tonight but he's staying here with us."

"Good," Roseanna said. "Let's pick him up and go eat."

"Now, young lady, about going out into a crowd like that." Maurice said sternly.

"I feel a lecture coming on," she said laughing, but she didn't mind. Tonight had been a success and she was happy.

Later on the way back to Nashville, Roseanna sat on the couch in the back of the bus, away from the noise of the engine, and out of earshot of Maurice, who was singing, slightly off key, stanzas of Amazing Grace. Michelle was napping in one of the bunks. Roseanna needed a quiet place to look over the script. She read it with interest.

Bayou Girl could have been a movie of her life; a young girl from the bayou makes it big in Nashville and is soon rolling in money and fame. As she read the pages it was almost like seeing her life unfold before her. It was as if someone was looking over her shoulder and recording everything they saw.

"All I have to do to make this movie is to be myself," she said. "Surely I can do that."

Her mind wandered to her father. It had been hard leaving him behind in Vegas, but that's the way he wanted it. He had promised to keep in touch and she knew he would. He had made her promise not to tell anyone she'd found him. He didn't want his family to know until he could go back home to them a whole man. Reluctantly, she had promised. She wanted to shout it from the rooftops, but she would abide by his wishes.

She forced her mind back to the script. By the time they rolled into Nashville, she had finished it and had decided to make the movie. She put the script aside and freshened up. It was good to be home again. She hopped off the bus and ran into the arms of the prince. He showered her with kisses.

"I missed you," she whispered.

"I missed you, too, baby," he said, kissing her again. "How did things go in Hollywood?"

"I won't tell you, I'll show you," she said excitedly. "Maurice, where are those newspapers?"

"Right here," he said, handing them to her.

She showed the articles to the prince. "All rave reviews," she said elated.

"Well, it looks like you didn't need me along at all," he pouted.

Roseanna laughed and told him the problems they'd had, taking the blame for almost being late for the concert. She told him what happened with the fans.

The prince frowned. "Baby, how many times have I warned you about that?"

"I've already gotten a lecture from Maurice, I don't need one from you," she said a bit huffy.

"I just worry about you, darlin'."

"I know and I love the way you take care of me," she said sweetly, realizing she'd been a little short with him. "I have wonderful news," she added.

"First, I've got to tell you something, baby, something not so wonderful. I wasn't expecting you home until tomorrow and I've got the guys coming over tonight."

"Prince, my first night at home, I was hoping we'd do something special."

"I'd like nothing better than that, darlin', but it's too late to call this off. This is our 'Wednesday Night Meeting of the Macho Men's Club'," he said flexing his muscles and smiling.

She laughed. "I wouldn't want to deprive you of that, but I'll miss you."

"I'll try to wrap it up early, baby. Now I've got a lot of things to do to get ready for the meeting."

"But I need to talk to you," she said.

"It'll have to wait, baby," he said, hurrying out of the room.

"Do we have a tour scheduled for January and February?" she yelled after him.

"No, not yet," he yelled back.

"I wanted to discuss this with him first," Roseanna mumbled, "but I've got to let Mr. Anderson know tonight. Oh well, Prince will be happy about it so here goes." She dialed the phone.

The prince introduced the men to her as they came in and then took them to his quarters to "play poker and shoot pool."

Roseanna was restless. She picked up the phone to call home, then hung up without dialing. She wouldn't be able to talk to Belle without blurting out the news about Daddy; she couldn't hide anything from her sister. Instead, she wrote letters to all of them, telling them how much she loved them and missed them. She wrote extra to Belle, telling her all about the trip to Vegas and Hollywood, not leaving out one little detail, except for the part about finding Daddy and that night in Vegas. She couldn't admit, even to Belle, that her Prince Charming was less than perfect. Then, exhausted from the trip, she sprawled across the bed and fell asleep.

She bounded into the kitchen the next morning where the prince and Maurice were drinking coffee. "I'm starring in a movie!" she exclaimed, all excited and bubbly, waving the script around.

"What did you say?" the prince asked alarmingly.

"I'm starring in a movie," she repeated.

"When did this happen?" he inquired a bit harshly.

"The night of the concert in Hollywood. Mr. Anderson, a producer, came to my dressing room after the concert. He offered me the lead in a movie called Bayou Girl and.."

"You did this behind my back, without my okay?" he stormed.

"I thought.."

"You don't get paid to think," he yelled. "I get paid to think. How dare you do this without talking to me first. I'm your manager and you only do something if I say you do it!" His face turned an ugly red, anger flashed in his eyes like that night in Vegas.

Maurice stood to his feet.

Maybe it was because Maurice was there, maybe it was because she'd done so well on her own in Hollywood, but for whatever reason, Roseanna was not afraid of the prince. She looked him straight in the eye.

"I know you're my manager. I tried to talk to you last night, but you were too busy. I had to make a decision and I made it. Now if you don't like it and want to walk—walk!"

The prince had never seen Roseanna in such a mood. He knew she meant it. "Whoa, baby, let's not fight about this. I'm sorry I got so angry. I'm concerned about your career. One wrong move could end it. Now let me see that contract."

"I don't have it," she said. "We made a verbal agreement over the phone last night. He's sending the contract..."

"You haven't signed anything?" The prince breathed a sigh of relief. "We're off the hook, darlin'."

"I gave my word."

"Your word's not binding, baby; your signature's binding."

"My word is as good as my signature," she assured him. "Besides, I want to star in this film and I'm going to—with or without you."

Maurice smiled and sat down.

"Can I at least see the script, baby?" the prince asked meekly.

She handed it to him and waited as he scanned through it.

"This actually looks pretty good, darlin," he said, much to her delight.

Roseanna spent the next day in Mavis's dress shop, trying on dress after dress. The state fairs were in full swing, and she was booked to do one-night-stands all over the country. She wanted to look her best.

"I'll take these," she said, handing several to Mavis. "I want them made up with mini-skirts and lower cut necklines."

Mavis gasped. "Are you sure about this?"

"Yes," Roseanna answered. "This is what my fans want."

"The men, at least," Mavis grunted.

"I have to give them what they want, Mavis. I'm dead as a singer without sex appeal."

"Did J.T. tell you that?"

"He knows this business," Roseanna said defensively.

"Maybe a little bit too well," Mavis grumbled. "Roseanna, you're a lovely young woman. You don't have to parade around half naked to have sex appeal."

"But I like to dress like this," Roseanna assured her. "I felt awkward at first but now I don't , so do I get my dresses done my way?"

"Against my better judgment," Mavis replied sadly. "You're playing with fire, Roseanna. I just hope you don't get burned."

"Don't worry about me, Mavis, I remember the talk we had. I'm not going to break the promise I made," Roseanna said, hugging her.

Roseanna received rave receptions at each fair across the country and when they were over, she knew for sure that she was the new queen of country music. She'd made it to the top—she had it all.

Once she got back home, she spent every free minute learning her lines for the movie.

It was Wednesday. "The fellows will be here soon, baby," the prince said. "Are you sure you don't mind being alone?"

"No," she told him. "It will give me more time to study my lines."

"How's that coming?"

"Good, so far. Of course, a little later I'll need someone to practice the love scenes with. Do I have any volunteers?" She winked at him.

"How many love scenes are in that thing?" he groused.

"Bundles and bundles," she teased, "but not to worry, after I've tasted your kisses, not even Romeo would stand a chance with me."

A knock at the door told them their guests were arriving.

Roseanna watched as they filed in: Al, a short bald man with an equally short temper; Bennie, a moody man, nice only when it suited his purpose; and Frank, who fancied himself a ladies man. The way he looked at her made her skin crawl.

"Macho men indeed," she thought. Then the newest member of the club walked in. Kent Abbott was a tall, sandy-haired man with a quick wit and ready smile. Roseanna had only seen him a few times but she liked him. She wished all of the prince's friends were more like him.

She was busy later, studying her lines, when Kent walked in the room.

"I had to get out of there for awhile," he explained. "Al's cigar—the way he puffs on that thing you'd think he had a smoke-stack in the top of his head."

Roseanna laughed. "I don't like people smoking in my house," she said, "but I hate to offend one of Prince's friends."

"Better one offended friend than four dead ones," he said jokingly.

"You're not like the rest of them," Roseanna told him. "There's something about you, Kent Abbott. Are you a church going man?"

He laughed. "I've been known to go on occasions," he said just as the prince walked in.

"It's your turn at the pool table," the prince said crossly. He went over to Roseanna and kissed her. "See you in a little while, baby."

"Bye," she said to both of them.

"What's that crack you made about church?" the prince asked when they were out earshot of Roseanna,

"She asked me if I went to church and I said I did sometimes. You want her thinking we're a bunch of heathens?"

"No, but don't talk that stuff with her. I had a hard time pulling her away from religion, and I don't want her thinking about it again. By the way, don't go getting any ideas about Roseanna; she belongs to me."

"Cool it, man," Kent replied. "I was just talking to her, I wasn't trying to seduce her. Besides I don't see a diamond on her finger."

"Diamond or no diamond, she's mine, and don't you forget it," the prince said angrily. "Now let's get back inside."

"I'm going to duck in the bathroom and splash water on my face," Kent said. "Al's cigar is getting to me."

"Okay, but make it snappy," the prince huffed.

Kent wanted to slap the handcuffs on him right now, put him in a cell and throw away the key. But he had to bide his time. His assignment here was far too important to jeopardize. He was after more than J.T. Prince; he was going to bring down the whole drug ring. He had to do it for Beth.

Tears stung his eyes as his mind flashed back to that painful night, four years ago: the loud and ugly fight between his younger sister, Beth, and their parents that had ended with Beth storming out the door, shouting insults at them. He had gone out looking for her, he searched all night but came up empty. The next morning, city workers found her body, crumpled in a dumpster. She had been raped and shot full of cocaine, then left in the dumpster to die. He was a cop and he couldn't keep his sister from ending up like that. He decided, right then, to work undercover, bringing down drug ring after drug ring until he found the man who killed Beth.

162

The FBI had suspected for a long time that J.T. Prince was involved in drug trafficking, but he was always one step ahead of them. They sent Kent in to get evidence against him and also to find out if Roseanna was a part of the drug ring. The bureau knew everything there was to know about her: where she grew up, who her family and friends were, they knew about Brad, and about her life since she moved to Nashville, but there was no way they could know if she was a part of the drug ring without someone on the inside observing her actions. At least that part of his assignment was over. He now knew for certain that Roseanna was in no way involved. She didn't know what went on in those weekly meetings. Like Beth, she was an innocent victim. He hadn't been able to keep his sister from dying, maybe he could keep Roseanna safe.

Tears welled up as a picture of his sweet, trusting, fifteen year old sister, lying dead in a dumpster, flashed through his mind. He renewed the vow he'd made to her that day, four years ago, standing over her lifeless body.

"I'll find the man who murdered you, Beth, if it takes the rest of my life. I'll bring down drug rings, one by one, until I find him and I will make him pay for what he did to you, I promise sweetheart."

He splashed water on his face. Someday, when the time was right, he would witness to Roseanna and tell her he was a Christian and try to convince her to go back home and marry her preacher; but for now, he had to go in there with that low-life scum and pretend he was one of them.

Chapter 15

The prince couldn't get Kent's words out of his mind. They sloshed around in his head like muddy pools of water. "No ring on her finger." So what if they weren't officially engaged, she belonged to him. She knew he loved her and that was enough, or was it?

Being alone in Hollywood had changed Roseanna, she was no longer that naïve little girl who looked to him for all the answers. That night in Vegas had brought him down a notch or two in her eyes. The way things stood now, could he be absolutely sure that she was really his?

"I'll make it official," he muttered, hurrying off to find her. "Baby," he called as she came down the stairs, "we're going out on the town tonight. I'm planning a big surprise so wear something special." He gave her a quick peck on the cheek and rushed out the door.

Roseanna stood there speechless. He had never left before without giving her a proper good-bye kiss. What was he up to?

She was alone in the house now. Maurice was running errands and the servants had the day off. She wasn't in the mood to do anything special, so she walked through the house admiring its beauty. It was every bit as elegant as Mrs. Pecot's house and twice as big. She looked at the massive chandeliers, glistening as rays of sunlight danced off them. She ran her fingers over the Rembrandts on the wall. She had everything she'd ever dreamed of; so where was the happiness that was supposed to come with them? These were the finest things money could buy; the best that life had to offer.

Roseanna sighed. These weren't the best things in life; she'd had the best things, back home on the bayou, when her heart was filled with joy instead of the emptiness she felt now.

"Snap out of it," she told herself, pouring expensive scotch whiskey from the bar the prince had set up in the den. "You're living the good life now. You're on top of the world. You've got it made, you *are* happy." She finished the glass of scotch and poured another.

"I'm just missing Belle, Mama, the girls and Grandma," and before she could stop it, her heart added Brad to the list. "I don't miss him anymore. I'm over him," she cried, trying to convince her heart.

"I'm home," Maurice yelled, walking in the door.

"Good," Roseanna whispered, putting a breath mint in her mouth. Now, maybe she could push those troubling thoughts from her mind.

Maurice didn't know anymore about the special surprise the prince was planning than Roseanna did.

"He's probably making up for my birthday, since we were touring the state fairs and didn't get to celebrate it."

"That sounds like J.T.," Maurice said.

"I'll have to find the perfect gown," she said, giving Mavis a call.

The prince stood at the bottom of the stairs that night, watching as Roseanna walked slowly down.

She looked lovely in a black, close-fitting, floor-length gown with sequins glistening here and there across the low-cut bodice. A slit in the skirt allowed ease in walking.

The prince's eyes feasted on her beauty. "Wow!" he whistled. "You look ravishing darlin'. Nothing on the menu tonight will be half as tasty as you."

"Thank you kind sir," she said, curtsying.

"Now for a fun-filled night of surprises," he said, helping her into his little red sports car.

Roseanna felt sure she was right about the surprise when the prince pulled into the parking lot of the same restaurant where he had brought her last year on her birthday. She took his arm and they walked inside. Tonight, the people didn't have to wonder who she was. "Roseanna!" they screamed, scrambling to get her autograph. The prince whisked her through the crowd and into a private dining room, the same one as last year.

"Prime Rib?" she asked knowingly.

"Yeah, how'd you know?"

"A lucky guess," she said coyly.

"I hope you don't mind, baby."

"I love Prime Rib and I love this surprise so far."

"This is just the beginning, darlin'. I promise this will be a night you'll never forget," he said, motioning to the waiter who was there to serve them.

After they finished eating, the waiter cleared the table and left the room.

"Let's dance," the prince said as soft music filled the room. He held her close as they danced to their favorite music, content to be in each other's arms.

"Let's sit this one out, baby," he suggested later, leading her over to the table. He opened a bottle of champagne and took her hand in his.

"Roseanna, I hope we have something to celebrate tonight. I'm crazy about you, baby. Thoughts of you fill my day. I dream about you every night. My life without you in it would have no meaning. What I'm trying to say is, I love you darlin', I want to spend the rest of my life with you. I know I don't deserve you but I'm asking you anyway: Roseanna, will you marry me?"

She was caught off-guard. She hadn't expected a proposal tonight, and what a grand one it was; candlelight, champagne, soft music, and those beautiful words.

Her mind flashed back to another proposal; one that was bungled and blurted out in front of the whole congregation, one that moved her to tears and made her heart sing. She had to put that one out of her mind, she had to focus on now.

"Baby, say something."

"I-I wasn't expecting this," she stammered. "I thought we were celebrating my birthday tonight. Your proposal overwhelmed me."

He took a diamond ring from his pocket. "Just say the word, baby, and I'll put it on your finger."

Her heart wasn't singing but she did love the prince. Her life was with him now. He did make her happy.

"Baby?"

"Yes, I will marry you," she said, holding out her hand while he slipped the ring on her finger.

He jumped up and pulled her into his arms. "Baby, you've made me the happiest man on the planet!" he exclaimed, kissing her. He poured champagne in their glasses and they toasted their

167

engagement. "Let's go home now, darlin', I've got another surprise for you."

They slipped out a back entrance to keep Roseanna from being mobbed again.

"Shhh, let's not wake Maurice," the prince said, unlocking the door of the mansion.

"Shouldn't we tell him our big news," she whispered.

"We'll do that tomorrow. Come with me, I want to show you something." He took her hand and led her back to his quarters. "I got these in case you said yes," he said, handing her several brochures.

"What are these?" she asked.

"The makings of our honeymoon," he explained, "just pick out the place you want to go, baby."

"Hawaii! Paris! Rome!" she exclaimed. "They're all so incredible! I can't choose between them."

"Then we won't," he said. "We'll take a month long honeymoon and go to all of them."

"Can we?" she asked eagerly.

"Sure. I'm the boss, I'll make it happen," he promised. "Nothing's too good for my baby."

"That sounds wonderful," she sighed dreamily. "I can't wait."

"We don't have to wait, baby. We can start the best part of our honeymoon right now." He grabbed her and kissed her with a hunger that demanded to be satisfied.

She responded to his kisses with all the feelings that welled up inside her.

His kisses became rough, each one burning with desire.

She melted in his embrace as she felt herself being pulled into the turbulence of her emotions. She was intoxicated, not from the champagne, but by the passions that raged inside her and she wanted to be his completely.

The promise she'd made flashed through her mind and she pulled away from him. "No, Prince, Stop!" she cried. "We can't do this, it's not right!"

"That was before, baby. You're wearing my diamond now, we're engaged, that makes it okay."

"No," she said, resisting his onslaught of kisses. "Engaged is *not* married."

"Same as," he retorted. "What possible difference can a few words before a preacher make?"

"All the difference in the world," she replied. "Our marriage vows make us one and only then do we have the right to each other."

"Don't be an old fogy," he sneered. "That kind of thinking went out with the hula-hoop. Get with the times, baby."

"Time won't change the way I feel," she told him firmly. "And besides, it's not only the way I feel, it's one of God's commandments..."

He snorted. "You've broken most of the other commandments, I don't know why you're so hung up on keeping this one."

"Prince, the promise I made is right. It's important to me, and I'm not going to break it, no matter what you say, and that's final."

"That promise is getting in my way," he said furiously. "You're mine, baby, and I want you now!" He pushed her down on the couch.

Roseanna shoved him away forcefully and stood to her feet. "Stop it!" she screamed. "You know how I feel about this. It's wrong and I'm not going to do it!"

"Only losers and nobody's think that way," he ranted in disgust.

She looked him straight in the eye and declared angrily: "I'm not a loser and I'm not a nobody but I am a virgin and I'll stay a virgin until the day I marry!"

He stormed out slamming the door behind him. Roseanna heard the tires squeal as he spun out of the driveway.

Tears filled her eyes. Had she made a mistake, was he right? Had she been wrong to make that promise? Should she have given in to the passions they felt? Did the ring on her finger make it okay? Had she driven him away forever with her out-dated ideals? Her mind was muddled. She didn't know the right or the wrong of it anymore.

As she pondered these things it was as if someone flipped a switch that turned on a light in her head. She could see clearly now; she was not wrong. But how could she make him understand?

She poured scotch from the prince's private stock into a glass and went to her room. She dressed for bed but she couldn't sleep. Her thoughts troubled her. Could they get beyond this, or was it over between them? Would he ever understand how important it was to her to stay pure until marriage? She was still pacing when the darkness gave way to dawn's early light.

She went downstairs to make coffee. The front door opened. The prince walked in looking disheveled and still wearing his tuxedo.

"Prince," she gasped, "you didn't come home last night?"

The color drained from his face. He had to think quick. "No, baby, I couldn't bear the thoughts of spending the night here, so close to you and not be able to hold you in my arms so I stayed in a hotel," he explained nervously, hoping she believed him. She must never find out where he really spent last night.

170

"I'm sorry about the fight," she cried , running into his arms. "I didn't mean to hurt you."

"Have you changed your mind about that promise you made?"

"No," she said gently. "That promise is a part of who I am. If I break it I would be throwing away a part of myself and I won't do that. I only hope you can understand and accept my decision so we can get beyond this and go on with our plans."

"I'll never understand it, baby, but I will accept it if that's the way it has to be."

"Thank you," she said giving him a kiss. "I do love you, you know."

Maurice walked in, yawning.

Roseanna held out her hand. "We're engaged!"

"Yeah, I can see that," he said smiling. "That's some rock on your finger, Miss Roseanna."

She nodded happily. "Maurice, since I'm almost a married woman now, can you call me Roseanna? Miss Roseanna makes me sound like a kid."

He laughed. "I'll try," he said. "Now when is this wedding?"

"I'd like nothing better then to go down to City Hall this afternoon and tie the knot," the prince answered.

"Nothing doing," Maurice said. "Miss—I mean—Roseanna's wedding is going to be done right."

"Yeah," she agreed. "This will be my one and only wedding and I want it to be something to remember."

"Okay, I see I'm outnumbered," the prince conceded. "Just make it as soon as possible, please."

"We've got the Christmas Special on CBS in late December," Roseanna commented. "We're filming the movie in January and February. I'll need a month or so after that to put the finishing touches on the wedding plans. How about April first?"

"April Fool's Day?" Maurice asked shaking his head.

"No, that won't do," she said. "How about March the thirty-first?"

"That's fine," Maurice answered.

"It's okay with the groom, too, if anyone's interested," the prince said in a pouting tone.

"I'm sorry," Roseanna said, putting her arms around him. "We didn't mean to leave you out. March thirty-first it is; mark that date on your calendars, gentlemen, as a red-letter-day—the day I become Mrs. John Taylor Prince."

"Let's seal it with a kiss, baby, and then I've got to be going. I've got a lot to do before the meeting tonight"

Kent arrived early for the meeting that night.

"You're the first one here," Roseanna told him. "Prince is not home yet. Come sit in here and talk to me."

"Wow! Look at that diamond," he exclaimed. "I guess that makes it official, huh?"

"Yes," she said excitedly. "The wedding is set for March thirty-first and you're invited."

Kent couldn't bear the thought of that slime touching Roseanna. He bit his tongue to keep from saying something. He could only pray that she would change her mind before the wedding.

"Kent, are you married?" she asked bluntly.

"No, I've never taken the plunge."

"Is there a special girl in your life?"

"Negative again," he told her.

The wheels in Roseanna's head spun into action. "I've got just the girl for you," she said, smiling.

"I'm not much for blind dates," he said, feeling nervous.

Roseanna laughed. "You're not getting off the hook that easy," she told him. "Besides the girl I've got in mind is a cross between a ballerina and a model. You two are perfect for each other."

"I don't know," he said, still hesitant.

"Nonsense," she said. "I'll call Mavis and set it up for New Year's Eve. We'll be back from New York City by then and we'll all ring in the new year together."

"Do you have a concert in the Big Apple?" he asked.

"No, a Christmas Special on CBS," she explained.

"I'll be sure and watch it," he said. "And it's okay about the double-date, too."

It was Christmas Eve and things were buzzing back home on the bayou. Roseanna had bought Mama a big screen television along with a satellite so they could watch the Christmas special. Brad was there. He'd go to Mississippi tomorrow to spend Christmas with his family but tonight he had to be here with Roseanna's family watching her on TV. It wouldn't be like seeing her in person, being able to reach out and touch her, but at least he would get a glimpse of her. For the first time in over a year, he'd see her beautiful face. They munched on Christmas goodies and sipped hot cider as they waited for the program to begin.

"Roseanna!" little Ellie cried as the spotlight outlined her sister standing there, ready to sing. "Pretty Roseanna," she muttered kissing the television screen.

Tears flowed freely from all of their eyes as they put hands on the screen, touching Roseanna's face.

"Sweetheart," Brad whispered painfully, as a hunger to hold her in his arms gnawed at his insides.

The emerald green gown Roseanna wore highlighted her natural beauty. She glowed as she sang "O Holy Night" to perfection. As she finished the song, the diamond on her finger sparkled, reflecting in the beams of the spotlight.

Brad winced when he saw it. He walked into the kitchen. Belle followed.

"I'm sorry, Brad," she said, putting her hand on his arm. "I know you still love her."

He nodded, forcing back the tears. "I've got to get over her, Belle. She'll soon be a married woman. I no longer have the right to love her this way."

"How did things get so messed up?' she cried, wiping tears away. "I'd like to shake some sense into that sister of mine, I'd like to tell her how much she's hurt you."

"Please Belle, don't ever let her know that I still love her," he pleaded. "Above all, I want her to be happy. I don't want her feeling any kind of guilt over me. I love her too much to cause her one moment of anguish. She's made her choice, let's not spoil it for her."

"Bradley Lefourche, you're one in a million," Belle sobbed. "Roseanna's a fool not to see that."

"I've got to get out of here," he said. "Tell your family good-bye for me. I'm leaving for Mississippi now instead of tomorrow. I'll see you after the holidays. Have a merry Christmas." He kissed her on the forehead and bolted out the back door.

Belle stood there weeping after he left. She felt his pain as if it were her own. Her heart ached for him. Would things ever be right in his world again?

Chapter 16

Bayou Girl was harder to film than Roseanna ever thought it would be. The glamour she expected wasn't there, just a lot of hard work.

Up before dawn, she began her day on the set, taking care of "behind the scene" things that had to be done before the day's shooting could begin, such as wardrobe, make-up, and rehearsing her lines for the day.

It was even worse when the camera started rolling; butterflies fluttered in her stomach, the bright lights bothered her, she forgot her lines and cringed each time the director yelled for a retake when she failed to heed one of his commands. But perhaps the hardest thing of all, was trying to play the role of someone so much like herself. When she tried to act natural, it came across sounding fake.

She might have given up altogether if not for Mr. Anderson, the producer. He believed in her. He hired the best teachers to help her with her acting. He was there on the set counseling her and giving her moral support. After about a hundred retakes and almost half as many acting lessons, she got the hang of it. Except for a few minor bobbles, the rest of the filming went as smoothly as any Hollywood production could go and they finished on time.

Roseanna was home now, exhausted, but pleased with herself. Even the director had complimented her on a job well done. Mr. Anderson had all but assured her, speaking from his years in the business, that the movie would be a box office hit.

The prince walked in, interrupting her thoughts, and giving her a friendly kiss on the cheek.

"Come here, you," she said. "I think we can do better than that." She put her arms around him and kissed him. He kissed her back in his own special way.

"That's more like it," she told him. "I missed you so much."

"I missed you too, baby. I'm sorry you had to go to Hollywood without me, but I had a lot of work to do so that we can take that month long honeymoon we've planned."

"I understand," she said, "and speaking of that, we need to go over our wedding plans to make sure we don't miss anything."

"I reserved the big cathedral down town," he told her.

Roseanna frowned. She wanted to get married in the little church back home with all her friends around her. She felt certain Brad wouldn't show up, but if he did, he could see how happy she was.

"I also called Reverend Barclay Claybourne. He's going to do the wedding for us."

Roseanna couldn't keep quiet about that. "Prince, I want Brother Trosclair to perform my wedding, not some stranger."

Reverend Claybourn is the biggest name in the religious world," he pointed out. "That makes him the perfect choice to perform our wedding."

"What's wrong with Brother Trosclair?" she snapped.

"Not a thing, baby," he quickly replied. "He's just not well-known enough. Our wedding's gonna be the news of the century. We need someone renowned like Reverend Claybourne"

"Well, getting married *is* the most important thing here," she said. "We'll do it your way."

"Thanks, baby, it'll be great, you'll see."

"Now, we need to get ready for the double-date with Mavis and Kent," she reminded him. "I hope things go as well between them as it did on New Year's Eve."

The prince scowled.

"It's an honor to be in the company of the two most gorgeous ladies in the universe," Kent remarked that night at dinner.

Roseanna and Mavis beamed, smiling warmly at him.

The prince fumed inwardly. That guy really got under his skin. Charm oozed from him like slow-running molasses. He was chock-full of charisma. Con all the way, but with his innocent looks and art of persuasion, he fooled everyone into believing he was the epitome of honesty. These qualities made him invaluable to the drug ring but irritated the prince to no end.

"If you gentlemen will excuse us, we're going to freshen up," Mavis said as she and Roseanna stood up to leave the table.

"J.T., I've got to hand it to you. This deal that's going down tomorrow night is going to make us all rich," Kent said when the ladies were out of earshot.

"It's the deal of a lifetime," the prince agreed, pleased with himself. "It took months of planning but it will mean hundreds of millions of dollars to us."

"The big man that's coming in from Detroit, do you know him?" Kent asked cautiously. He had to tread lightly here. J.T. must never suspect that he's trying to get more information than what he would normally need to know.

"Only that he goes by the name of Mr. Black, which is not his real name; he's called that because he always dresses in black. And I know he's big in drug trafficking, but he needs connections, which we can supply. I've also heard he's mean as a rattlesnake."

"Do you expect trouble?" Kent inquired.

"No, but bring your gun just in case."

"What about Roseanna, will she be in the house?"

"Of course not!" the prince snapped. "Don't worry about Roseanna, I'll take care of her. Mavis is picking her up, and they're going out for a night on the town."

"Good thinking, J.T.," Kent said as the girls rejoined them.

The rest of dinner went smoothly and they all had a good time.

"Baby, is your father coming to the wedding to walk you down the aisle?" the prince asked when they got home.

Roseanna's mind flashed back to the week-end she spent with her father in Vegas when she was making the movie. She asked him to give her away at the wedding.

"No!" he exclaimed emphatically. "I'll never give my little girl away to that smooth talking snake-in-the-grass!"

She couldn't tell the prince that so she told him a half-truth. "No. He's not ready to face Mama yet and I don't want to postpone our wedding until he is ready, so

I asked Maurice to give me away. He's been like a father to me since I've been here in Nashville."

"That's great, baby. I'll find someone else to be my best man."

"I'm sorry, Prince, I wasn't thinking. Of course you'd want him to be your best man."

"Being a substitute father for you takes top billing over being my best man," he said. "I'll get one of the guys.."

"What about Kent?" she blurted out. "Mavis is my maid-of-honor, along with Belle, and we have been spending time with them. Please say yes," she pleaded.

The prince cursed under his breath. The last person in the world he wanted standing up for him on his wedding day was Kent Abbott, but could he deny Roseanna this one thing after she'd given in to all his other demands concerning the wedding.

"Okay, baby I'll ask him," he promised grudgingly.

"That takes care of all the major plans for the wedding," she said. "Just think, in a couple of weeks I'll be Mrs. John Taylor Prince." She snuggled in his arms and they sat talking about the plans for their life together until the wee hours of the morning.

The next day, Roseanna sat staring at the blank sheet of paper before her. She wanted to write a love song to sing to the prince at their wedding, but the words wouldn't come. She thought of her love for him, she remembered the good times they'd shared, all the beauty he'd brought into her life. She visualized their life together as man and wife—still no words, no melody. She put down the pen and paper.

"The wedding is so formal he wouldn't want me singing to him anyway." She sighed wearily, giving up on the whole notion.

The prince paced nervously. Tonight the big deal was going down. Had he planned it out well enough? Were his bases all covered? There was no room for error here. He mulled over the details of the drug deal itself, it was all in place, it was solid. He went though his plans to make sure everyone except the drug dealers would be out of the house tonight.

The servants had the night off. Maurice would leave for church around seven o'clock, Mavis would pick Roseanna up by seven-thirty. The big man from Detroit would arrive at eight. Everything was planned like clockwork; nothing could possibly go wrong.

Roseanna walked in taking his mind off of tonight.

"Baby, I'm not sure I want you going out alone, looking like that," he said, wishing he hadn't ordered her jeans two sizes too small.

"What's wrong with the way I look?"

"Nothing darlin', that's the problem," he said. "Every man out there will be eyeing you and I'll be stuck here with the guys, crazy with jealously."

"We could change our plans and stay here and smooch," she teased.

"Believe me, baby, I'm tempted."

"How about one for the road?" she said, moving into his arms and kissing him just as the doorbell rang.

The prince opened the door. Al, Bennie, and Frank filed in.

"Where's Kent?" he asked.

"He's driving his car tonight," Al replied, "said he was going to see a girl later."

"I'm here," Kent said, bounding up the steps and through the open door.

"Hello, Roseanna," he said, flashing a big smile.

"Thanks for being Prince's best man," she said.

"Happy to, that way I'll be the first to kiss the beautiful bride, with the exception of the groom of course," he teased, knowing full well that if things went as planned tonight, there would be no wedding. The FBI would move in; J.T. Prince and the others would be carted off to prison. Then he would be free to witness to Roseanna about the Lord and maybe help her get back on track with her life.

The prince frowned. He had to get that Casanova away from Roseanna. He kissed her. "I'll wait up for you, baby," he said, taking the men to his quarters just as Maurice walked in on his way to church.

"Maurice, was Prince ever in love before?" Roseanna asked pointblank.

"Why do you ask, child?"

"I'm just curious. He's never mentioned being in love but there must have been someone special in his life before I came along."

"Yeah, about ten years ago there was a special girl in his life. I thought they would get married. They seemed so much in love but then all of a sudden it was over between them. I never knew what happened."

"Who was she?"

"I'd rather not say," Maurice told her.

"Come on, tell me," she coaxed.

"Ask J.T. he'll tell you."

"I want to know now. I'm not letting you out this door until you tell me her name," she threatened playfully.

"J.T. should be the one to tell you," he said hesitantly.

"I can't live one minute longer without knowing who she is. Please tell me," she pleaded.

Maurice could see there was no getting around it so he gave in. "It's no big secret, it was Mavis," he said walking out the door.

Mavis—ten years ago. Roseanna's head reeled, her knees felt wobbly, she got sick to her stomach. "No," she gasped, "it can't be, not Prince. He wouldn't do that; he wouldn't kill his own baby; he couldn't be that heartless. It has to be a mistake." But she knew it was true, Maurice wouldn't lie. It all made sense now, Mavis warning her about the prince. Dear, sweet Mavis, trying to protect her from the man who had hurt her so badly.

Roseanna was in no shape to go out. She dialed the phone. "I can't go tonight," she said, when Mavis answered. "I've got a splitting headache. I'm sorry to spoil our plans."

"That's okay," Mavis said sympathetically. "Get some rest and I'll talk to you tomorrow."

Roseanna couldn't rest, she had to keep moving. It felt as if a thousand sticks of dynamite were exploding in her head as her dream world crumbled around her and she stood there in the shattered pieces of her life. She could never forgive the prince for what he did to Mavis and their unborn baby. Now he had destroyed her life as well. She had loved him; she had trusted him; she had even given up her soul to please him. How could she have been so wrong about him?

"Oh, Brad," she cried, reaching out for that haven of safety she once felt in his love. "You were right about him, but I wouldn't listen. I found out too late that my prince is a frog in disguise, and I'll pay for that mistake for the rest of my life."

She felt herself choking. She ran to the front door and opened it, gasping as she took in big gulps of the brisk March air.

The four men walking up to the mansion startled her. Panic seized her as she realized she was alone, here, except for the prince and his friends, and they were at the other end of the house.

The big man in black spoke in a gruff voice: "Is this the residence of J.T. Prince?"

She nodded.

"We're expected," he said walking in the door. The other three followed.

Trembling, she showed them to the prince's quarters.

What were men like that doing here? she pondered. Why was the man in black carrying a suitcase? Why didn't the prince tell her about them? A chill went up her spine as she thought about people like that being in her house.

The man in black rapped sharply on the door. The prince opened it and stepped back in surprise. "I didn't hear the doorbell, how did you get in?" he asked.

"That great looking babe let us in," the man said gruffly.

"Roseanna," the prince gasped under his breath. What had gone wrong? Why was she still in the house?

"We're here to deal," the man said. "Let's see what you've got."

Kent's heart sank within him. All hell was about to break loose. Roseanna would be caught right in the middle of it, and there was nothing he could do to stop it. He shuddered to think what would happen if these men resisted arrest.

The prince stood there, stunned momentarily, thinking of the danger he'd put Roseanna in. If anything went wrong with the deal tonight, what would the man do to her, to all of them?

"Are we dealing or not?" the man snarled.

"I'm ready," the prince said, anxious to get it over and get these men out of the house.

"You have connections with the Colombian cartel, right?" the man said. "I'd better not be wasting my time on a small-time operator."

"I've got all the connections you'll ever need ," the prince assured him. "My connections go all the way to the top."

"You'd better be for real," the man threatened.

The prince nodded to Frank. He brought the cocaine over for the man to see.

"Good stuff," the prince said, "over 80% pure."

"I'll be the judge of that." The man snapped his fingers. One of his men walked over and touched a small amount to his tongue. He nodded.

"There's a hundred kilos here; worth millions, on the street, and there's plenty more where that came from," the prince told him.

Kent eyed the door, hoping for a chance to slip out and warn Roseanna. The FBI would move in soon and they didn't know she was in the house. He had told them her plans to be out for the night.

"Hey, you," the man in black said, looking at Kent, "don't I know you?"

Kent shrugged. He had to stay calm. He tried to remember if he'd ever seen the man before. "No, I don't think so," he answered truthfully.

"He's one of my key men," the prince explained, "moved here from California."

"I could swear I'd seen you somewhere," the man insisted.

"I've got that kind of face," Kent said, passing it off lightly. He had to play it cool, there'd be no chance for him to warn Roseanna now. He could only pray for her safety.

The man in black kept staring at Kent. A knowing look came over his face. "I remember you now, from the newspaper clippings of the funeral. Your kid sister OD'd on cocaine. Such a pity, she was a pretty little thing, and spunky too. She fought me like a tiger at first but then the cocaine took effect and we had a high ole time.."

"You! You filthy swine!" Kent cried out mournfully. "You killed Beth!"

"You're right, you dirty cop, but not til I had a night of sleazy fun with her," he smirked.

"I'll kill you with my bare hands," Kent raged, lunging at him.

"No, I'm gonna kill you, you low-down Narc." He drew his gun and aimed it at Kent.

"No boss," one of his own men shouted, bumping his arm, but too late. A shot rang out and Kent crumpled to the floor.

The man in black turned and glared at his man with a cold, hard steely look in his eyes.

"Please, boss," the man pleaded. "I was only trying to help. You know what they do to cop killers."

"I know what I do to traitors," he said, shooting the man straight through the heart. He fell to the floor a few feet from Kent.

In the confusion that followed the prince bolted out the door and ran down the hall. He grabbed Roseanna's hand and pulled her out the door, running towards his little red sports car.

"Run, baby," he cried. "They'll kill you!" He shoved her in the car, jumped behind the wheel and spun out towards the pasture.

"Get the girl!" the big man ordered. "Where's that Prince fellow?" He looked around. "That sorry scum's got the girl. Find them and kill them !"

He looked at Al, Bennie, and Frank.

185

"We're with you," they said trembling, joining in the search.

At that moment Brad arrived at the secluded cabin in the woods in South Mississippi. He was facing the toughest battle of his young life—getting over Roseanna. He had to erase all the love for her from his heart. He couldn't do it on his own, his love for her was imbedded deep inside him. He didn't want to let go of it, but he had to. In a few days she would belong to another man and these feelings he had for her would be sinful. He had come to this deserted place where there was no way of communicating with the outside world, there was no telephone, no radio, no TV and no one around for miles. He would not be disturbed here.

This cabin, on his grandparent's farm, had been his special hide-away when he was a boy and wanted to be alone to face some problem or just to think. He needed this place of refuge now, more than ever. A place he could to try to mend his broken heart, to pick up the pieces of his shattered life and try to go on. If only he didn't love her so much; if only his heart would release him to love again. He couldn't even imagine living the rest of his life without her. His love for her had not waned one bit in the months they had been apart. He needed help getting over her and God was the only one who could help him. He had a two weeks vacation and he'd spend every minute of it right here, alone with God, seeking His face and praying to forget Roseanna.

As he stood there in the dimly-lighted room, a feeling of doom swept through him. "Roseanna," he whispered and fell to his knees.

"Oh Father, God," he prayed, his heart throbbing with fear. "Roseanna's in trouble, I know it. I can feel it in every fiber of my being. I can't be there with her, Lord, but You can. Father, watch over her, shield her from this harm that's so close to her. I love her with all my heart, Lord, but I'm not asking you to send her back to me, I'm only asking You to please watch over her, take care of her in the midst of this danger. I ask You, Father, to wrap her up in Your Arms of safety and love, and keep Your mighty Hand on her."

Tomorrow he would pray to forget her; but tonight he sensed that she needed the strength of his love.

Chapter 17

"Where are we going?" Roseanna shouted hysterically.

"We've gotta get out here, fast!" the prince yelled.

"But we're out in the pasture," she yelled frantically.

"I know what I'm doing, baby," he said trying to assure her. "I found a pig trail through here one day when I was out riding. It's not much but I can get my car over it. It leads all the way to the main highway and I'm the only one who knows about it."

"But they'll see our lights," she cried.

"Not if we can make it around that bend ahead. We'll be completely out of sight and they'll never find us."

"I'm scared," she whimpered.

"Don't worry, baby, I'll get us out of this. Hold on, it's a bumpy ride."

"His car's gone," Bennie reported to the man in black. "They're making a run for it."

"Quick, into the cars," the man ordered. "We'll follow them down the mountain. Shoot him on sight, but save the girl for me, I want to have some fun with her before I kill her."

They froze as a voice boomed out loud and clear. "You, inside the house, this is the FBI. Lay your weapons down and come out with your hands over your heads."

"The Fed's," the man in black snarled. "Come in and get us," he yelled, breaking a window and firing in the direction of the voice.

"Lay your weapons down and come out with your hands raised," the voice boomed again.

The other drug dealers started shooting.

Chief Bristol, head of the FBI team, gave the order to commence firing. A barrage of bullets whizzed through the air.

The drug dealers fell like flies until only Al, Bennie, and the man in black were left standing. They refused to surrender.

"Let's go get them," Chief Bristol yelled. "Be careful where you shoot, we don't want Kent caught in the crossfire."

They burst in, cautiously guarding each other's backs. They carefully made their way down the hall towards the prince's quarters.

"This is your last chance to surrender," the chief shouted. "Come out with your hands raised."

"I'll do to you what I did to your dirty, low-down spy," the big man yelled, opening the door and shooting randomly down the hall.

The agents returned the fire and he fell in a dead heap at their feet.

Al and Bennie walked out with their hands above their heads.

"Get that slime out of here," the chief said, hurrying over to where Kent lay in a pool of his own blood. He knelt beside him.

"Kent," he said somberly, "it's chief Bristol. Hang in there, son, help's on the way." He held on to

Kent's hand tightly as if to give him strength to hold on to life.

"Man—in—black," Kent gasped, "he—killed—Beth."

"He'll never hurt anyone again, he's dead," the chief said. "You got him. Beth can rest in peace now."

Kent winced in pain as a slight smile etched his face. "I—did—it. I—brought—him—down—for you—Beth. I—made—him—pay."

"Save your strength, son," Chief Bristol urged."

"Roseanna—is" he gasped again, trying to let them know she was in the house.

"She's not here, remember," the chief said reassuringly. He choked back the tears as he felt Kent go limp in his arms. "Someone's going to pay for this ," he vowed. "Where's J.T. Prince?"

"We've searched the house, there's no one here. His car's gone too," one of the agents replied.

"We had both roads leading out of here blocked. How did he get away?"

The agent shook his head.

"Throw a drag-net over the city," Chief Bristol ordered. "Find the location of every piece of property Prince owns within a hundred mile radius of Nashville. I need this information on the double and I don't care whose cage you have to rattle to get it. J.T. Prince is coming down."

The prince and Roseanna sat in silence as the car bumped across the pasture, into the meadow, through the woods, and down to the main highway.

"We made it, baby," he sighed in relief as they turned onto the highway and sped away, careful to observe the speed limit.

"What happened back there?" Roseanna asked trembling. "I heard gunshots."

"That man in black went crazy when he saw Kent, he knew him from before. There was an argument and he shot Kent."

"No!" Roseanna cried, horror-stricken. "Not Kent—is he dead?"

"I didn't stick around to find out, baby," he answered. "I had to get you out of there. That man would have killed you too—both of us,"

"But why?" she sobbed.

"He's mean darlin'. He killed one of his own men for trying to help Kent. Besides we can identify him; he can't let us live."

"Will he find us, are we going to die?"

"No, baby," he said, putting his arm around her. "I've got a cabin near here. We'll be safe there."

"I don't think I'll ever feel safe again," she said, snuggling over to the prince, needing the comfort of his closeness.

"Relax, baby, I'm gonna take care of you," he promised, pulling her close to him and holding on to her tightly.

"Why did this happen? What was that horrible man doing in our house?"

"We'll talk about it later, baby," he said. "I need to get us to safety right now."

He was buying time. How could he ever tell Roseanna the truth? Curse that Kent Abbott, this was all his fault. Served him right—getting killed like that. Thanks to that low-down snoop, the FBI now knew everything about him and the drug operation. They would be hot on his trail when Kent's body was found. He'd get the blame for all of this. He had to lay low until he could get out of the country. He turned off the highway onto a winding dirt road.

Roseanna turned on the radio. She sat back and listened to soft music hoping it would calm her nerves.

"We interrupt this program to bring you some late-breaking news," the announcer said. "Our reporter is on the scene."

"Baby, you don't want to hear this," the prince said nervously, trying to turn it off.

She stopped him. "I want to hear it. It might be about Kent."

"I'm here at the home of Roseanna LeBlanc, well-known star of country music, where a large amount of cocaine was seized earlier tonight in a drug bust. The FBI moved in and shots were fired. There are several confirmed deaths, no names are being released at this time."

Roseanna sat there, dazed, unable to move.

The reporter continued: "An APB has been issued for J.T. Prince, a prominent Nashville business man, suspected of being the leader of the drug ring."

Roseanna turned off the radio. "No," she gasped, the color draining from her face. "It's a mistake! Tell me you didn't do this," she screamed, beating him with her fists.

"Stop it, Roseanna!" he shouted. "You're going to kill both of us!" He shoved her away roughly. "Get over there and shut up!"

She sat huddled against the door, whimpering, like a little puppy who had just been kicked by a master who was supposed to love it.

They arrived at their destination a few minutes later. The prince parked the car, out of sight, in a clump of tall bushes behind the cabin.

"Stop your whining and get out of the car," he ordered.

"No!" I won't go with you," she shouted.

"I don't have time to argue with you," he scowled, reaching for her.

"Don't you dare touch me!" she yelled, kicking and screaming as he picked her up and carried her into the cabin.

He slammed her down on the bed and glared at her angrily. "Don't fight me on this, I'm trying to save your life!"

"It's because of you that I'm in this danger!"

"Don't put all the blame on me," he fumed. "I had it worked out; you were supposed to be out of the house tonight. You were supposed to be with Mavis."

"Mavis," she gasped. With all else that happened tonight, the memory of Mavis and the baby had been pushed completely from her mind.

"What kind of man are you?" she cried with a contempt that she had never felt before. "A drug dealer, a liar, a murderer.."

"I'm not a murderer!" he shouted. "I didn't kill Kent."

"I'm not talking about Kent," she sobbed. "I'm talking about your baby."

"I-I don't understand," he muttered.

"Mavis—the abortion," she said coldly.

"Oh, that."

Roseanna shook her head in disbelief. "It means nothing to you. You killed your own baby and you don't even care."

"That was a long time ago," he stated. "I had my whole life before me. I didn't want to marry Mavis and I didn't want a kid. I was too young to be strapped down with a family so abortion was the only answer. Besides, it wouldn't have been fair to the kid to bring him into this world under those conditions."

"Is that your excuse?" she screamed. *"You* were too young. *You* didn't want a kid. Why didn't you think about that *before* you made the baby? Not fair to the child, you say? Was it fair for you to become judge

193

and jury and condemn your child to die, without giving him a chance at life? Did you ask him if he wanted to live—no, you made that choice for your baby because you didn't want to be tied down!" Roseanna's stomach was churning around like a whirlwind. She ran to the bathroom and threw-up. She stayed there awhile to try to calm down. How could she have loved such a monster? He was walking in the door, talking on his cell phone, when she came out of the bathroom.

"Steve, I'm in a bind. I need your help. I need to get out of the country."

"Sure, man, where are you?"

"I'm at the cabin. Do you think you can fly the plane in tonight?"

"That depends. Is everything the same as it used to be?"

"Yeah, it's the same as we left it. I just checked it out."

"I don't see a problem. I can be there in four hours."

"Thanks, Buddy," the prince said, putting down the phone. "That was a friend of mine, baby. Years ago, when I first moved to Nashville, we found this place. I bought it and we built a runway in a clearing a few yards from the cabin. We outlined it with reflectors so he could see to land at night. That was necessary in our business."

"Drugs, no doubt," she said sarcastically.

The prince ignored the remark. "He'll pick us up here in a small plane and take us to his jet. He's filing flight plans as we speak. No one will suspect a thing. We're going to make it, baby."

"I'm not going with you," she said flatly.

"Yes, you are. I'm not leaving you here to be hunted down by those drug dealers."

"I'll take my chances," she told him.

"As soon as we're in another country we'll go ahead with our plans to be married," he said, ignoring her again.

"I'd rather face the drug dealers than to marry you," she cried.

"That's okay by me," he said. "I'm not the one that's hung up on being legal. I thought it was important to you, but married or living in sin, you're mine baby, and when we get to where we're going, I'm going to have you, legal or not—the choice is yours."

"I'm not going and you can't make me!"

"You can either walk out of here on your own two feet or I'll carry you, but you *are* going and that's final."

"Prince, please, I want to go home. I haven't seen my family in two years. I miss them so much."

"I'm your family now, baby, and you're mine," he said. "I'll miss Maurice too, he's like a father to me. There's some things I'd like to tell him before we leave but I can't. I don't want him feeling guilty over the way things turned out. It was my choice to get involved in drugs. If there's any good in me, it's because of him. I'd like for him to know that, but I can't chance calling him. The FBI will be listening in to all calls." Tears misted his eyes as he spoke of the kind, gentle man who had practically raised him.

He does have a little bit of a conscience, Roseanna thought, seeing the tears. He did have good in him, she'd seen that, too. She had learned to love him because of that goodness; she had agreed to be his wife because of it. She would appeal to that good side of him now.

"Please," she pleaded, "let me call Mama, they'll be worried sick. I need to let them know that I'm okay and when I'll be home."

"You will never go home again," the prince told her. "Our life in this country is over. We can never have contact with anyone here again. I'm sorry, baby, but you've got to forget your family; you've got to cut all ties forever."

"No!" she screamed, "I won't! I can never forget my family. I love them! Please don't do this."

"Your place is with me. You're wearing my diamond; that's commitment, baby."

She yanked the ring off her finger. "Here, take it back!" she yelled, throwing it in his face. "I want to go home!"

"Never!" he shouted.

Roseanna sobbed as she thought of the safety back home and the joy of being in the bosom of her family. Panic gripped her as she faced losing that forever. She remembered Brad's strength and the security she'd felt in his arms.

"Oh, Brad," she cried out. "Help me, please, help me!"

The prince whirled around and back-handed her across the mouth with a force so strong that it sent her tottering backwards across the bed. He hovered over her, rage flashing in his eyes.

"Don't ever mention that man's name again!" he stormed. "You belong to me now and don't you ever forget it. Now get some rest, we've got a long night ahead of us."

Roseanna knew there was no need to argue. She lay there quietly, hoping for a chance to escape. If he dozed off for just a moment she could make it out the door and into the woods. She could hide until the plane arrived, he'd never chance losing his only ticket out of here to look for her. As the night wore on, exhaustion overtook her and she fell asleep.

"Wake up, baby," the prince said, gently shaking her. "The plane's here."

Pure terror seized Roseanna as she heard the plane's engines overhead. She crouched at the foot of the bed, crying, as the prince reached for her.

"No, please," she begged. "I can't do this, please don't make me go with you. If you love me, please leave me here, let me go home."

"Home for you now is with me, baby, so let's get going. We're on a tight schedule." He dragged her off the bed and across the floor, releasing his grip on her when the voice rang out.

"J.T, Prince, this is the FBI. You are surrounded. Come out with your hands over your head."

He cursed and grabbed his gun.

"No, Prince, don't!" Roseanna cried. "You don't stand a chance! They'll kill you!"

"I'm too close to freedom to give up now," he exclaimed.

"This is you last chance," the voice boomed over the loudspeaker. "Come out with your hands over you head."

"Please, Prince, I don't want you to die. You'll go to prison, but at least you'll be alive. Please do as they say."

"No!" I'll never give up," he ranted. "I'll shoot my way out!" He grabbed her and holding her in front of him for a shield, he started towards the door.

"No!" she screamed, fighting to pull loose from the grip he had on her. It was no use. She was no match for his strength.

"Please Prince," she begged, "don't do this." Her plea's fell on deaf ears.

He reached the door, opened it, and started shooting.

197

Roseanna felt a supernatural surge of strength go through her. She wrenched free of his grasp and lunged sideways.

The thunderous explosion of bullets filled the air and Roseanna heard the thuds as they hit their target and the prince crumpled to the floor.

"No," she gasped, then she felt a burning, tearing pain in her side as steel ripped through flesh. Her knees buckled, a soft whimper escaped her lips. The room spun and she felt herself hit the floor. Voices, sounding faint and off in the distance, fell on her ears as the FBI burst into the cabin.

Chief Bristol looked grim as he walked in and saw her lying there. "Roseanna," he muttered. "I don't understand. She's not supposed to be here. Kent tried so hard to protect her and now we've shot her." He felt her wrist. "There's a slight pulse. Quick, get those medics here on the double!" He pressed his handkerchief on the wound to try to stop the bleeding.

The room was hushed, somber. Federal agents are supposed to be tough, but tears filled the eyes of these men as they stood by helpless, watching the life ebb from her body. They bowed their heads in silent respect for the young girl who had become America's sweetheart.

As Roseanna lay there in a pool of blood, it was as if she was transported back in time; to that little white church back home. The whole congregation was gathered there, smiling and happy. Brad was there tenderly holding her hand. She wanted to hold on to his hand forever and never leave this place, but she felt herself being pulled away from him, from all of them, slipping into a deep abyss. Brad tried to hold on to her but she slipped from his grasp and fell headlong into the abysmal chasm. She knew she was dying. Her heart cried out in anguish, and for the first time in years Roseanna found the strength to pray.

"Oh, Jesus," she cried, "don't let me die now. I've got one song left to sing," and in a voice barely more than a whisper she sang: "Amazing Grace, how sweet the sound, that saved a wretch like me." As she sang, Roseanna felt that Amazing Grace flow through her like a pure cleansing fountain , washing away years of guilt and shame, and peace filled her heart.

The men standing round joined in and sang in hushed tones.

The room started spinning, the voices became as echo's bouncing off the walls, the sound of approaching sirens grew faint, the pain in her side lessened, a coldness crept over her and darkness engulfed her like waves of dense fog rolling in over the water. Total darkness consumed her and she faded into nothingness.

"We're losing her!" Chief Bristol cried.

"Hold on, Roseanna," a young agent said, gently stroking her forehead.

"Where are those paramedics?" the chief shouted.

"Oh God, please don't let her die," the young agent prayed.

Through the thick maze of darkness Roseanna felt a strong Hand holding hers, a comforting Hand, a loving Hand. She felt strength pulsating through her from the touch of that Hand. A blinding light encompassed her and a warmth saturated her entire being. The Hand tenderly caressed her wounded side and gently lifted her to her feet.

Chief Bristol grabbed hold of her. "No, Roseanna, don't try to stand."

The paramedics came running in.

"Over here," the chief yelled, helping them get Roseanna on the stretcher. He turned to the medics.

"She's lost a lot of blood. A minute ago we thought we'd lost her."

"We'll take a look," they told him.

One side of her clothing was soaked with blood. They carefully cut it away; her side was covered with blood.

The tall thin medic who was in charge rubbed his gloved hand over the entire bloody area. He rubbed the other way. He nodded to his assistant. The young medic examined her side. They looked at each other.

"Where did you say the wound was?" the tall man asked in a puzzled tone.

"You've got your hand on it," Chief Bristol answered in an even more puzzled tone.

"Bring me a wet towel," the first medic said to his assistant. He carefully washed the blood away. "This woman was not shot," he declared.

"You're crazy, man," the chief snorted. "We saw the hole in her side where the bullet penetrated. We saw the blood pouring out of the wound."

The other agents nodded; they had seen it too.

"The bullet must have grazed her, knocking her to the floor and she fell in his blood. That's the only possible explanation," the medic insisted as if he hadn't heard them.

"This is her blood," Chief Bristol exclaimed, pointing to one pool of blood, "that is his blood. You can see where he fell; you can see where she fell!"

The medic stood his ground. "There's no way she could have been shot. Come take a look." He motioned to the chief.

Chief Bristol looked at her side. It was smooth, free of any wound, not even a scratch was there. "I don't understand this, but I know what I saw," he huffed.

"I know what I *see*," the medic said. "You can't argue with facts: there's no wound; she was not shot."

"I saw it with my own eyes!" the chief declared angrily.

Roseanna listened as they argued. "Gentlemen," she said, "I can clear this up." She turned to the medics. "These men are right. I was shot. I felt the bullet as it tore into my side. I knew I was dying. I prayed and asked Jesus not to let me die; I remember singing Amazing Grace. I felt a joy flow through me and everything went black. The next thing I remember a strong Hand was holding mine and a bright light was shining around me. I felt a warmth go through my body and that Hand tenderly caressed the wound in my side, then the Hand lifted me to my feet. Gentlemen, the answer is simple; I was healed by the Hand of God!"

"You were hallucinating," the young medic piped up. "Things like that don't happen in the real world."

"Chief Bristol, you other agents, do you know for sure that I was shot? Did you see the wound in my side, did you feel it?"

They nodded. They had seen it; they had felt it.

"There was a wound, now there's not a wound; explain that if you can," Roseanna challenged them.

They stood quietly, not uttering a sound. The young agent smiled, knowingly.

"You are men of logic," she continued. "Logic sees and believes. You have seen a miracle here, gentleman, so logically you must believe it."

The men stood there bewildered, not able to comprehend what they had just witnessed, but how could they deny what they had seen?

Kent used to talk about stuff like that," the chief said somberly.

"Kent was a Christian?" Roseanna blurted out joyously.

"Yeah," Chief Bristol said. "He was always trying to get us to change our ways."

"Some of us listened," the young agent said.

Roseanna's attention turned to the prince lying on the floor. She ran over to him. She fell down beside his lifeless body and cradled him in her arms. "Why, Prince, why?" she cried in a voice filled with pain. She wept hysterically.

"We've got to take him now," the tall medic said, compassionately, helping her to her feet.

"I'm going with you," she sobbed, getting into the ambulance. There were no sirens, no flashing lights, just an eerie silence which said it all; death was here and there was no need to hurry.

Maurice was at the hospital, waiting. Roseanna ran into his arms and they wept together, mourning the loss of a man they both loved, the waste of a life that had held so much promise.

Finally, Roseanna spoke through her tears. "Maurice, when this is all over, please take me home. I need to be with my family."

Only there in their loving care would she feel safe again.

Chapter 18

As the big white limousine headed out of
Nashville, Roseanna turned and took one last look at
the city that had been home to her for almost two years.
She'd had good times there; she would miss it.

She was riding in the front of the limo with
Maurice. Neither of them wanted to be alone with their
thoughts.

She sighed. "Maurice, I feel like I'm a hundred
years old."

"I don't wonder, child," he said tenderly,
"you've been through more these past two weeks than
most folks go through in a lifetime."

The past two weeks had taken their toll. She'd
been cleared of any guilt in the drug ring, thanks to
Kent, but he had paid with his life. She owed her
freedom to him and now she could never repay him.

In spite of everything the prince had done, his
death hit her hard. It wasn't easy forgetting the special
things about him: the way his eyes twinkled when he
smiled, how he looked in a tuxedo, the things he'd done
just to make her dreams come true, the good times
they'd shared, all their special moments together.
These memories were fresh in her mind and seemed to

over-ride the bad times. Today would have been their wedding day if things had not gone so terribly wrong. Roseanna couldn't keep back the tears as she thought of all their beautiful plans, now shattered along with the rest of her dreams.

The funeral had been private, just a few close friends. Chief Bristol and some of his men were there along with some local officers who kept the curiosity seekers away.

Roseanna and Maurice clung to each other and wept bitterly as they said good-bye to the prince for the last time. It was hard to walk away and leave him there alone. Roseanna set up a fund so that fresh flowers would be kept on his grave at all times. His must never become a forgotten grave, as if no one cared.

Roseanna was stunned to find out the prince had put everything in her name. She cringed when she thought of how he had acquired these ill-gotten gains and the lives that had been ruined because of it. She didn't want anything that had even the hint of drugs attached to it. She used the money to set up a drug rehabilitation center to help kids kick the drug habit; maybe that way she could make up for some of the wrong he'd done. She put all of his property on the market with the proceeds going to the center.

She signed the recording studio over to Harriet. It would thrive in her capable hands.

Roseanna had been back to the mansion only once since that night. The prince's presence was overwhelming, everywhere she looked, memories of him lingered. She wept as his voice rang in her ears: "Baby, I love you." How many times had he whispered those words to her as he held her in his arms and kissed her.

Her heart had never been free to love him wholly, but she had loved him in a special way. She never would have kept her promise to marry him once she found out the truth, but she couldn't forget him either. Standing here, amid all these memories, in spite of everything, she longed to see him one more time, to be in his arms and feel his kisses, to hear him whisper, "Baby, I love you."

"I can't stay here," she cried, running from the house. She could never live here again, but she didn't want to sell the mansion. She wanted it to count for something; she wanted good to fill the rooms that had held so much evil that night.

After talking to Mavis, she donated the mansion with all of its furnishings to be used as a home for wayward girls. There they would not only receive the care they needed, but counseling and guidance as well, so hopefully they would not make the same mistake Mavis had made. If they could help save the lives of innocent babies, maybe it would make up, in some small way, for that life that had been snuffed out because of the prince's selfishness. Mavis would be the administrator, making sure everything ran smoothly. Roseanna donated all her jewelry and gowns to be sold, with the money going to help fund the home.

That took care of all her business in Nashville and it was time for Roseanna to leave. She said a tearful good-bye to Mavis, Michelle, Harriet, and the guys in the band. She would miss them, but she had to go home. The same yearning that had pulled her away from the bayou was now pulling her back there.

"Oh, Maurice," she cried as these memories tore her apart, "Will our world ever be right again?"

"I hope so child," he said, choking back the tears.

"I know you miss him so much," she said, putting her hand on his arm.

Maurice nodded. "He was like a son to me," his voice broke, "but somewhere along the line I let him down."

"No, Maurice, you didn't," Roseanna cried. "That last night he was thinking of you and he wanted you to know that getting involved in drugs was his choice and no fault of yours. He said if there was any good in him, you put it there and we both know there was good in him."

"Thank you for telling me that, Roseanna. I'll be a long time getting over his death but maybe now the guilt will ease a little."

Early, the next morning, as they drove down familiar roads leading home, Roseanna feasted her eyes on the beauty around her, a beauty she'd never noticed before.

"Maurice, I'm almost home," she sighed happily, then a worried look crossed her face.

What would home be like now? Could she handle being there, so close to Brad, knowing that his arms that once held her, would now be holding someone else? What a fool she had been to give him up. She winced, remembering their love, so pure and tender. She had never gotten over him; she never would, but she had to put up a good front. He must be free to love the new girl, totally and completely, without any guilt over her. This would be her gift to him.

What was she like, this new girl who had taken her place in Brad's heart? She must be special for Brad to choose her to share his life.

A tear slid down Roseanna's face, She had to talk to Brad alone one more time. She had to let him know that he was in no way second best to the prince; that he was the strongest man she'd ever known and he could never be second best to anyone. She'd tell him this and then fade out of his life forever. She would become just one of the congregation to him and he'd be her pastor; nothing more.

Roseanna's heart leaped with excitement as they turned onto the dirt road that led to the church. It was after ten o'clock, so the service would be underway. She dreaded going in, Brad's new love would be there. Belle had told her about Molly and now she had to come face to face with her. She had to smile and pretend she was happy. She had to wish her well. Her stomach was queasy thinking about it. She'd sneak in the back and get a good look at her before she had to face her. She'd be easy to spot, she'd be the girl wearing the locket.

"I'm going to take a nap," Maurice said, getting into the back of the limousine. He'd driven all night to get her here in time for church this morning. He needed to rest.

Brad stepped out of the parsonage just as Roseanna started toward the church. She stopped dead in her tracks. Their eyes met.

He ran to her, pulled her into his arms and kissed her with all the love that was in his heart. She kissed him back and it was as if they belonged in each other's arms, as if they'd never been apart.

Brad stepped back in horror. "Roseanna, I'm sorry," he gasped. "I don't have the right to do that."

Yesterday was her wedding day. She was a married woman and he had kissed her.

Roseanna understood. He was committed to someone else, he might already be married. Her heart was breaking; that kiss felt so right but it was so wrong.

"Late again, Reverend Lefourche," she teased, trying to clear the air between them.

He smiled, remembering. "No. I'm on vacation," he explained. "I came back a day early and thought I'd go over and hear Brother Trosclair's message."

She wondered if he'd been on his honeymoon, but she didn't ask. She couldn't bear to hear those words from him. Instead she said, "Do we have time to talk before you go in, there's something I want to tell you."

"Sure," he said. Was she going to tell him she was married? Did she think he didn't know?

"Can we go to my special place?" She needed the haven of that place to find the courage to be close to him and not fall to pieces.

Brad's thoughts were troubled as they walked toward the bayou. He'd never question God's way, but he didn't understand. He'd prayed so hard these past two weeks to forget Roseanna. Why didn't God answer his prayer? Why did she have to come by here instead of going directly to her storybook honeymoon. He understood she'd want to see her family after being gone so long, but why now? And why did kissing her feel so right?

They reached her special place and she turned to face him. "Brad," she started, then hesitated. She thought the words would come easy here, but they didn't. How could she make him understand how special he was without blurting out that she loved him.

"Brad," she started again. "I'm sorry about the way things turned out. I want you to know that even though I agreed to marry the prince..." Tears welled up in her eyes.

"It's okay, Roseanna," he said, not wanting to hear about the prince and her.

"No, I've got to say this, you've got to know. Brad, even though I chose to marry the prince it wasn't because he was more of a man than you or that he was better than you in any way. You're the strongest man I know, Bradley Lefourche and you could never be second-best to anyone. I came here to tell you that."

His voice choked. "Thank you, that means a lot to me and for you to interrupt your honeymoon to come tell me means even more."

"My honeymoon?"

"Yeah, I know yesterday was your wedding day."

"You don't know?" she blurted out. "It's been all over the news."

"I've been at the cabin on my grandparent's farm in seclusion for the past two weeks. I haven't heard any news."

"The prince is dead," she sobbed.

"No," he gasped and took her in his arms. "I'm sorry Roseanna, I didn't know."

Cradled in his arms she told him the whole story; about the drug ring, how the prince was killed, how she was shot, and then healed by the Hand of God.

"I should have been there for you," he said, holding on to her tightly.

She felt safe in his arms. She wanted to stay there forever but she didn't belong there anymore, someone else did. She pulled away and ran off towards the bayou.

"Wait, Roseanna, don't go," Brad yelled, running after her. He caught up with her and took her in his arms again.

"No!" she cried, trembling. "I can't do this! I can't stay here close to you, knowing you love someone else, seeing you with her. I want you to be happy, Brad, but I can't stay and watch you share your life with someone else."

"Roseanna..."

Not giving him a chance to speak, she went on, blurting out the very thing she was determined to keep from him.

"Brad, I know you don't love me anymore, and I don't blame you. I treated you shamefully, leaving you the way I did. I've never stopped loving you and I never will. I tried so hard to forget you after you wrote that letter."

"What letter?" he interrupted.

"The letter you wrote thanking me for setting you free from the promises we made. I didn't mean that letter, Brad, it tore my heart out to write it. I loved you so much I didn't want you to feel tied down to those promises. When you wrote back and said that we were never meant for each other and that you had found someone else, it broke my heart. I couldn't believe you would write a letter so cold and unfeeling."

"I never wrote a letter like that," he assured her.

"It was your handwriting," she cried.

"The letter I wrote said that I loved you and would wait for you forever."

"I never saw a letter like that.'' She paused. "Someone must have switched—but how?"

"Forgery," Brad said, his jaw twitching angrily. "The prince must have somehow forged the letter and then he destroyed the real one."

"How could he do that to me? How could he hurt me that way?"

"He wanted you for himself so he had to tear us apart," Brad said, his jaw twitching again.

"It worked," she cried. "When I read that letter, my heart broke inside me, I felt lost and alone. You were my strength, Brad, and when I lost you, I had nothing to hold on to. I got carried away in that other world and did things I'm not proud of. I turned to the prince when I thought I had lost you but I didn't give in to his desires—I almost did—I came so close…"

"Did he force himself on you?" Brad demanded furiously.

"No," she said, tears streaming down her face. "It was me, too—I knew it was wrong—but I almost let him—I wanted to—but I didn't, Brad, I didn't. Thank God, I didn't!" She wept hysterically in his arms.

"Shhh, sweetheart, it's okay." Brad consoled her like a tender shepherd would console a lost little lamb. "You're here now and that's all that matters."

"No, because of the prince, I've lost the only man I'll ever love. Of all the things he did to me, this was the worse; making me believe that you didn't love me anymore. Now you don't love me—you love Molly—Belle told me."

"Roseanna, listen…"

"I don't blame you for loving her, you deserve to be happy…"

"Roseanna," he said, trying to get a word in.

"The locket—it was once a symbol of your love for me, now Molly's wearing…"

Brad put his hand over her mouth. "Listen to me, Roseanna," he said. He pulled the locket out from inside his coat. "I took this with me to the cabin and I prayed for two weeks with it clasped in my hand, because I knew in my heart that it could only belong to one girl and she was about to marry someone else." His voice broke. "I prayed so hard to forget you, but God didn't answer my prayer. Now I know why. This is the only place the locket will ever belong," he said, putting it around her neck. Tears were streaming down his face as he stood there holding his beloved Roseanna in his arms.

"What about Molly?"

"Belle only told you that hoping to make you jealous. She never gave up on you and me."

"You still love *me*?" she asked tearfully.

He pulled her close and kissed her with a tender passion. That was all the answer she needed.

211

Her pulse was racing, her heart was singing. "I'm glad to be back home in your arms where I belong," she whispered, kissing him with all the love overflowing inside her.

Memories of the prince, good and bad, vanished from her heart as she stood there in Brad's arms, safe and secure in the strength of his love.

Later, they would talk about that night when Roseanna's life was in jeopardy, and realize that Brad was on his knees, for the whole seven hours that she was in danger, praying for God to keep His Hand on her. But right now, they were content to be in each other's arms and only spoke of their love.

One month later the little white church was adorned in all it's beauty. The fragrance of roses filled the air as folks gathered into the sanctuary. It was Brad and Roseanna's wedding day.

Roseanna , looking radiant in her beautiful gown, waited in the parsonage, along with Mavis. Belle had taken the other girls over to the church to make sure they were in their places when the ceremony began.

"Thank you for coming so far to share my special day with me," Roseanna said embracing her friend.

"I'm pleased that you asked me to be your maid-of-honor, along with Belle," Mavis replied. "I'm happy things worked out for you and Brad."

"Isn't he wonderful?" Roseanna sighed, with stars in her eyes. "Someday, you'll meet Mr. Right and I'll be coming to your wedding, as your maid-of-honor, of course."

"Of course," Mavis laughed. "Now, let's get this veil on you and get you ready to walk up the aisle."

"Roseanna." The man spoke her name softly.

Roseannna's heart skipped a beat. She stopped breathing. That voice, so very familiar. *But he's dead,* she thought. Her mind raced to retrieve reality. She whirled and looked at him. The color drained from her face, she stumbled backyards. He reached out and caught her. She touched him, felt him. He was real. "You're alive," she gasped. "But how?"

"Only by the Hand of God," he told her.

"I don't care how it happened, I'm just glad you're alive!" she exclaimed. She threw her arms around him. "If not for you, I wouldn't be here today marrying the man I love. I owe my freedom and my happiness to you, Kent Abbott, and I'm forever in your debt," she cried, tears streaming down her face.

"Come on, now," he said, misty-eyed, "we can't have you crying on your wedding day." He kissed her on the forehead.

"I don't understand—on the news—they said you were dead."

"They said an undercover agent had been killed. Everyone thought it was me so we left it that way to protect the families involved."

"Who then?" she asked, puzzled.

"You remember the man in black and his men— you let them in that night."

She shuddered, remembering.

"It's a long story but that man recognized me and pulled his gun to shoot me. One of his men bumped his arm…"

"And the man killed him. Prince told me."

"I didn't know it, but that man was an undercover agent too. When he found out that I was a fellow agent, he tried to save my life and died because of it. You talk about owing a debt to someone—I owe that man my life and I'll never get to thank him." Tears were flowing down his face. "Because of his bravery, the bullet missed my heart by a fraction but it was enough to save my life."

"Why didn't you let us know you were alive?"

"I had to lay low until the FBI wrapped up the full investigation which led all the way to a cartel in Nicaragua. There were still some bad guys around who knew me, so the director thought it would be best if they assumed I was dead for awhile. You should have seen their faces when they walked into that Grand Jury room and saw me; they all pled guilty on the spot," Kent explained. "I needed a place to hide out during this time and this gorgeous lady took me in and took care of me."

"And you didn't tell me?" Roseanna scolded, looking at Mavis.

"She was sworn to secrecy," he explained again. "We didn't know if this would be cleared up in time for me to make it to the wedding, so we had to keep it quiet. Everything was finalized last night so I jumped in my car and here I am." He pulled Mavis into his arms and kissed her.

"Something going on here that I should know about?" Roseanna asked.

Kent grinned. "Yeah, I asked her to marry me and she said yes."

"Kent has taught me to trust again and to love again," Mavis said. "And it's all thanks to you, Roseanna, and that blind date you talked us into."

"Shows what a good matchmaker I am," she said, beaming.

"This beautiful lady has made me want to settle down and have a family, so I gave up undercover work and took a position as vice detective for the Nashville PD."

"I'm so happy," Roseanna cried, hugging them.

Maurice tapped on the door. "It's time," he said, drawing back in horror when he saw Kent.

"It's okay, Maurice, he's not a ghost. We'll explain later, but now I've got a wedding to go to."

Mavis and Kent walked on ahead.

"Maurice, thank you for being my stand-in Dad," she said taking his arm.

"I wish your real Dad could have been here but since he's not, it's an honor to stand in for him."

The music started. The attendants marched in and took their places at the front of the church.

Little Ellie started up the aisle, taking each step slowly, carefully scattering flower petals as she walked. She smiled at the folks sitting on each side of her as she made her way to the front. This was her big moment and she was making the most of it.

"I believe this is my job," a voice said.

Again, Roseanna's heart skipped a beat. It leapt for joy within her as she turned to look into her father's smiling face.

Maurice flashed a big smile and stepped aside. "We prayed you'd make it on time," he said.

Roseanna took a deep breath. "Daddy, I'm glad you're here to give me away," she said, tears misting her eyes.

"I'll gladly give my little girl to that fellow standing up there. It's because of him that I'm here today. I called Maurice, and wanting to surprise you, your young preacher persuaded your mother to talk to me on the phone and we're working things out. He also rented this tux for me in case I made it on time."

Little Ellie made it to the front and strains of "Here Comes the Bride" pealed forth loudly. The guest stood and faced the door. They stood in silence as Roseanna started up the aisle, awe-stricken by her beauty.

Grandma almost fainted when she saw Ellis LeBlanc walking beside his daughter. Mama tapped her shoulder and nodded that everything was okay.

"Who gives this woman to be married?" Brother Trosclair asked when they reached the front.

Ellis LeBlanc reached out and took his wife's hand. She stood up beside him. A special look passed between them.

"Her mother and I do," he said tenderly, placing Roseanna's hand into Brad's waiting one.

Sobs filled the sanctuary as the guests wiped tears from their eyes. It was as if two marriages were taking place today: one being restored after years of separation, one about to begin.

Brother Trosclair nodded to Roseanna. She took Brad's hands and looked into his eyes. "Brad, your love means so much to me; it fills my heart to overflowing. I've written this song to express some of the ways that I love you"

Her band played the melody and she sang from her heart.

Like apples of gold, in settings of silver,
Like raindrops that turn into rivers of wine;
Like a soft wind moves cross a high green meadow,
Like a ruby that glows, babe, like a diamond that shines;
Like a candle that burns with a slow certain passion,
Like the call of a dove from a tall oak tree;
Like cherries in bloom at the end of December,
You belong in my heart, babe, glad to have you with me.

Like a bird on the wing in a sky of pure splendor,
Like a river that rolls into regions unknown;

Like a long country road leading to someone
tender,
Like a wayward child finally turning back home;
Like a candle that burns with a slow certain
passion,
Like the call of a dove from a tall oak tree;
Like cherries in bloom at the end of December,
Well, always remember, babe, I'm glad to have
you with me;
Always remember, glad to have you with me,
You belong in my heart, babe, glad to have you
with me.

After the song ended Brad smiled lovingly at Roseanna then spoke tenderly, words from his heart.

"Roseanna, I loved you the first time I saw you, I love you today and I will love you for all of my tomorrows. You are my inspiration. You give me strength to soar above the ordinary and reach for the stars. You're the wind beneath my wings. I could never be complete without you by my side, and I will cherish you all the days of my life."

Then, after repeating the traditional vows and exchanging wedding bands, they heard the words they had waited so long to hear.

"I now pronounce you husband and wife. Bradley, you may kiss your bride."

Brad's and Roseanna's hearts were filled to overflowing as they shared their first kiss as husband and wife, then amid shouts and applause they ran down the aisle, holding tightly onto each other's hands. Rice pelted them as they raced to the limousine and sped away to the Pecot mansion for the reception.

Mrs. Pecot had insisted that it be held there and she had gone all out to make sure it was a gala affair.

Laughter and merriment rang out as everyone dear to Roseanna and Brad joined in the celebration.

The afternoon wore on. It was time for the bride and groom to say their good-byes and head off for their honeymoon. Well wishes followed them as they drove away.

When they reached the parsonage, before going in to change for the long trip ahead, they walked hand in hand to Roseanna's special place. She felt drawn here today as she had so many times before. Standing on the brink of womanhood she wanted to come here, with her beloved Brad, to bid farewell to her childhood.

Roseanna's heart was singing as she stood there in Brad's arms looking at the beauty around her; so simple yet so priceless. She shivered as she thought of how close she'd come to substituting those "things" in that fake world for the "real things" right here. Her heart was filled with love and gratitude to the One who had given her a second chance at life.

"Thank you, God," she whispered.

She looked at Brad with love in her eyes. The journey back to him had been long and hard and there were times she doubted she'd ever make it; but here she was in his arms, about to embark on the first steps of their life together.

Standing there in that special place, as the setting sun cast shadows around them and the old alligators slept lazily in the marsh beyond, Brad kissed her. Her world was right again. Her heart was finally home.